D1715573

The Gilded Nightmare

THE
GILDED
NIGHTMARE

Hugh Pentecost

DODD, MEAD & COMPANY
New York

Published by Dodd, Mead & Company, Inc.
79 Madison Avenue, New York, N.Y. 10016
Distributed in Canada by
McClelland and Stewart Limited, Toronto
Manufactured in the United States of America
First Red Badge printing
Library of Congress Catalog Card Number: 68-21901
ISBN: 0-396-08447-8

Part One

1

"As of yesterday," I said, as casually as I could manage, "the Baroness Zetterstrom had one million dollars in cash deposited in a personal checking account in the Waltham Trust."

Chambrun's eyes twinkled at me from under their heavy lids. "You have some kind of prejudice against a million dollars, Mark?"

"But in a checking account!"

Chambrun looked down at a pink card on his desk. "Two four-room suites," he said, "and three intervening single rooms with bath. The two suites go at three hundred dollars a day apiece, and the three single rooms at sixty-five dollars a day each. That comes to seven hundred and ninety-five dollars a day without tips, food, liquor, or any other pleasures. The reservations are for one month. You think she can make it on a million?"

Pierre Chambrun is a small, dark man, stockily built,

with heavy pouches under bright black eyes that can turn as cold as a hanging judge's when he's displeased, or unexpectedly light up with humor. He's been in the hotel business all his life, and has reached the pinnacle of that profession as resident manager of the Beaumont, New York's top luxury hotel. He would, I think, be irritated at the suggestion that there might be a better hotel anywhere in the world. He might make a grudging concession to outer space, but he'd have to be shown. French by birth, he came to this country as a small boy, and he thinks now like an American. But his training in the hotel business has often taken him back to Europe, and he can adopt a Continental manner to please a queen. He's a brilliant linguist. I've never counted the number of languages he can speak fluently. The Beaumont is his world. He often says it's not a hotel but a way of life.

Somewhere in the distance, sunning himself on the Riviera, is Mr. George Battle, owner of the Beaumont, who presumably does nothing but count his money. He rarely interferes with Chambrun's management of the Beaumont, and when he does it's in the form of a humbly craved favor.

The Baroness Zetterstrom was one of those favors. "Anything you can do for Charmian Zetterstrom will be appreciated," Battle had wired Chambrun.

The next day one Marcus Helwig, who described himself as the Baroness' "steward," called from London and made the somewhat fabulous reservations—two suites, three single rooms. Without being asked, he'd provided

Chambrun with the Waltham Trust as a financial reference. It was routine to check out the reference and I'd produced the answer from the bank.

"Who in the hell is Charmian Zetterstrom?" I asked. A lady who tosses around that kind of money has to be someone.

Chambrun's face had turned hard and cold, an expression I rarely saw there when I was alone with him. He flicked the ash from his Egyptian cigarette. He seemed to sink a little deeper in the heavy armchair behind his exquisitely carved Florentine desk. He reached for the demitasse at his elbow and found it empty. I carried it across the thick Oriental rug to the sideboard, where his Turkish coffee-maker is constantly in operation. I filled the small cup and brought it back. His eyes were almost hidden behind the deep pouches.

"Baron Conrad Zetterstrom belongs in the black part in time," he said.

I knew what he meant by that. There had been four years out of his life when he'd fought in the French Resistance.

"A conniver, the king of the Nazi sadists, reported to have been a sexual deviate of the most extraordinary flamboyance. And rich. While Germany slowly lost its life, General Zetterstrom salted away a huge fortune in Swiss banks. After the war he escaped prosecution in the war crimes trials. Some kind of legal shenanigans. He bought himself an island in the Mediterranean and built what has been described as a Shangri-La that would have made the late William Randolph Hearst drool with envy. They say it was the Kingdom of Evil on earth. He died two years ago at the age of eighty-four. He left his entire empire to his widow, an American girl he married about twenty years ago. She was just out of her teens then—an unsuccessful film actress, rumored to be extravagantly beautiful, able to match the old man's taste for sadistic debauchery. Now she is the widowed Baroness Zetterstrom, come away from her island fastness for the first time since her marriage. She is still said to be breathtakingly lovely."

"What bothers you about her spending her money here?" I asked.

"That she may try to turn the Beaumont into a club for the international queer set."

"And if she does try?" I asked.

He looked at me as if I'd asked a totally absurd question.

"Out on the sidewalk on her seductive bottom," he said. . . .

On the eve of the arrival of the Baroness Zetterstrom I was in my third year as public relations director for the Beaumont. It says so on the door of my fourth-floor office—MARK HASKELL, PUBLIC RELATIONS. In the beginning I'd been feeling my way around in the job like an infant learning to walk, guided by Shelda Mason, my glamorous and agitating secretary, who'd worked for my predecessor and made me feel like anything but an infant.

For two years now Shelda and I had been teetering on the brink of matrimony, but the life we live is so exciting, so full of change and crisis and engrossing problems, that somehow we haven't taken the plunge. Actually, the hotel had become our life. Both she and I had what she calls "Chambrun fever." We felt possessive about the Beaumont. It was our town, with its own mayor in the person of Chambrun, its own police force, its own public services, its cooperatively owned apartments, its facilities for transients, its nightclubs, its cafés, its restaurants, its quality shops opening off the lobby, it complex human relationships.

Like Chambrun, Shelda and I had become jealous of the Beaumont's reputation. At the end of the official working day I found myself changing into a dinner jacket and spending the evening moving about from one bar to another—within the hotel—through the ballroom, the private dining rooms, the Blue Lagoon nightclub, the restaurants, making certain that the Swiss-watch efficiency of the place was in perfect order. Shelda says I'm like Marshal Dillon, checking out Dodge City every night. Sometimes she makes the rounds with me. Sometimes she goes to her little garden apartment a few blocks away and waits for me to join her. I live in the hotel myself, and Shelda's place is the only "hideout" I have from the buzzing activity of the Beaumont's world. Of course Chambrun knows where to find me; and Jerry Dodd, the hotel's security officer. We don't have anything so lowbrow as a "house detective" at the Beaumont.

7

On that night before the arrival of the Baroness, things were so orderly at the Beaumont I should have been forewarned that it was some kind of lull before a storm. I wasn't. I was particuarly hungry for Shelda that night and I took off for her place shortly after eleven o'clock. The golden-blond love-of-my-life was wearing an enticing, pale-blue negligee, under which was only Shelda. She was poring over a collection of fashion designs which were part of the plan for a couturier's show she was running for me the next day. A pair of shell-rimmed glasses were perched on the end of her nose. I am the only person who's ever seen her wearing glasses. Woman, thy name is Vanity.

She waved toward the kitchenette and said: "On the rocks for me."

I went, and came back with two double Scotches. She pointed to a little package, gift-wrapped, on the edge of her work table.

"For you," she said.

The presents we give each other, except on major occasions like Christmas, or any day I'm particularly in love, or vice versa, are usually jokes. I opened the package and found in it, folded in tissue paper, a pair of the black eye-patches that people sometimes wear to keep out the light when they're trying to sleep.

"How come?" I said, preparing for the joke. "I only have insomnia when I'm lying very close to you, angel, and then I like it."

"They are for you to wear when the Baroness Zetterstrom appears on the scene."

I grinned at her. "She's that torrid?"

Shelda scattered the drawings on her desk and produced some newspaper clippings. They were from the London *Times*. There was a photograph of the Baroness arriving at Shannon Airport about ten days earlier. The picture showed a small, dark, svelte woman surrounded by an army of retainers. She couldn't possibly be forty. I said that.

"The photograph doesn't show the wrinkles that must exist at the corners of her eyes and around her neck," Shelda said. "Why do you suppose she wears black glasses?"

"Bright sunshine."

"To hide the truth about her age," Shelda said. "You notice the young man standing just to her left? The one with the long hairdo? She pays him to service her—as we used to say down on the farm."

"How do you know?"

"Read the clippings," Shelda said.

According to the clipping, the young man was Peter Wynn, the Baroness' "secretary-companion." I guess that was polite-British for gigolo. The whole retinue wore black glasses. There was a tall, slightly gray-haired man with a thin, hard mouth that looked as if it had been sliced into his face, who was identified as "Marcus Helwig, legal adviser to the Baroness"; a short fat man called Dr. Malinkov, her medical resident; a blond Brunhilde called Mme. Brunner, personal masseuse to the lady; Heidi, a pretty

German-looking girl who was described as "personal maid," and in the background a lean, tweedy man with a kind of tense look to him, who was described as John Masters, bodyguard.

"I wish they weren't coming," Shelda said.

"Why?"

A little shudder happened under the blue negligee. "Woman's intuition," she said. "That bitch spells trouble."

I quoted Chambrun on what would happen to the lady if there was any touble.

"Why does he wait till after the fact?" Shelda said. She got up and went away into the bedroom.

"Perhaps because she has a million bucks to spend," I said. "That's the first entry on her personal file card. Deposited yesterday in the Waltham Trust."

No answer.

"To hell with the Baroness," I said.

"I'm way ahead of you," Shelda called to me.

There is a secret card-index file at the Beaumont that would drive a professional blackmailer out of his greedy mind. Every client, past or present, is recorded in that file, and most of them wouldn't have been pleased at how much the Beaumont knew about them or how they were evaluated by the staff. There is a code system used on the cards that tells a great deal more than the name, address, and marital status of the customer. Under "financial" there are three ratings—1, 2, and 0. The 0 arbitrarily stands for "over his head," meaning that that particular guest can't afford the Beaumont's prices and shouldn't be allowed to get in too deep; 1 is for millionaire and 2 for the just very rich. The code-letter *A* means the subject is an alcoholic; *W* on a man's card means he's a woman-chaser, possibly a customer for the expensive call girls who appear from time to time, despite our efforts, in the Trapeze Bar; *M* on a woman's card means a man-hunter. *MX* on a man's card means he's double-crossing his wife, and *WX* means the woman is playing around. The small letter *d* means diplomatic connections. A lot of U.N. people make the Beaumont their headquarters. Governments can afford our prices where individuals often can't. If there is special information about a guest it is noted on the card. If that information isn't meant to be public knowledge in the front office, the letter *C* indicates there is information in Chambrun's private files.

On the morning of B day, which was how the day of the Baroness' coming was described by the staff, I took a look at the file cards covering the lady and her retinue. On the Baroness' card was simply the indication that she was a number-one credit risk and the letter *C*, meaning Chambrun had further information. The others were equally bare. The credit portion simply indicated that Charmian Zetterstrom was responsible for the lot of them. The sky was the limit.

"One million bucks worth of hell-raising," Mr. Atterbury said to me. He's the day reservation clerk who never refers to the card file because it is all computerized in his head. "If it wasn't for Battle's cable I don't think the boss would take them in." His smile was thin. "All connecting doors between the two suites and the three single rooms are to be unlocked. They'll be able to play musical beds in there without attracting attention."

"Do you care?" I asked.

Atterbury shrugged. "The rooms are soundproofed," he said.

You develop habits in my kind of job. At a quarter to one each day I go up to the Trapeze Bar for one very strong, very dry vodka martini on the rocks. One sets me up for what is apt to be the busiest part of the day for me; two make me sleepy. I don't go there just for the drink, but to see if there are any luncheon guests of special importance to the hotel's public relations—big-time politicos, movie stars, or someone newsworthy in the social swim.

But I enjoy the drink.

On B day I found a friend at the bar. I sat down beside him and signaled to Eddie, the bartender, for my usual. Sam Culver was in the process of filling a charred black-briar pipe from a yellow oilskin pouch. Sam is somehow what you expect from a chain–pipe smoker—easy going, philosophical, with a gentle humor. He's in his early forties, and he maintains a slim, muscular figure by careful eating and a daily workout in the Beaumont's gymnasium on the twenty-first floor. I think he plays squash almost every day. I made the mistake of taking him on one day. I'm younger and should get around faster and with more vigor than Sam, but he cut me to ribbons. He's a tactician of the first order. He managed to stay in front of me in center court and had me running from side to side and up and down until my tongue was hanging out. I understand the squash pro has trouble with him.

Sam is a writer. He made quite a lot of dough in Hollywood early in his career. He now writes a column which is syndicated three times a week across the country and around the world. Sam writes about people, gently, perceptively, amusingly. Gossip doesn't interest him. Each piece is a little nugget of character analysis. Many people are flattered to be the subject of one of his pieces. Not a few run at the sight of him. They know how clearly he sees through sham, the false front.

"Just the man I wanted to see," Sam said, after he'd got his pipe going. "Know your habits, so I was waiting."

"At last you're going to interview me," I said.

A cloud of blue smoke floated around his gently smiling face. "Believe it or not, Mark, I have a hatful of notes on you. The man who sees all and knows, surprisingly, nothing about what he sees."

It wasn't meant to be wounding. I didn't take it as a dig.

"Surface facts are your job and you're an expert at collecting them," he said. "Below-the-surface facts are my job. Harder to come by, but, I tell myself, more interesting. I am now, however, in search of a surface fact."

"Be my guest."

"Do you know what time the Baroness Zetterstrom is supposed to arrive today?" Sam asked. He nodded to Eddie, who'd brought my martini, indicating he wanted a refill.

"She arrives at Kennedy at two o'clock," I said. "If the

plane's on time and she buys her way through customs in a hurry, she should be here in the neighborhood of three o'clock."

He just nodded.

"You aim to do a piece on the mystery woman?" I asked.

He looked at me, his smile just a little tighter than normal. "Mystery woman? I knew Charmian Brown when she wore pigtails," he said. "Grew up with her. She's complex, but not mysterious."

"I didn't know anyone knew her. It's rumored she hasn't been off her island for twenty years. Zetterstrom brought the world to her there, according to Chambrun."

"The word is *bought*, not brought," Sam said, staring into his blue cloud of smoke. "I'm interested to see what all that has done to her."

"Made her perhaps the richest woman in the world," I said.

"There you go with surface facts," Sam said. "In my terms, it may have made her the poorest." He tamped down the tobacco in his pipe with his forefinger. "Know that fellow at the end of the bar?"

I looked. A tall, dark, good-looking man in a worn tweed jacket was brooding over a whiskey on the rocks. I guessed he was about Sam's age.

"Who is he?" I asked.

"Not a Beaumont regular?"

"I don't think I've ever seen him before."

Sam's smile grew tighter. "I don't think Charmian will

be pleased to see him," he said.

"Again—who is he?"

"His name is Stephen Wood," Sam said.

"Do I have to pry it out of you with a can opener?"

"Drama is uninteresting when it's explained in advance," Sam said. "But I suggest you watch the confrontation when it takes place."

"I have ceased being fond of you," I said.

"Oh, I'm playing it all very lightly, Mark. The cheerful smile hiding the cancerous growth." His face had gone rock-hard. He slid down off his bar stool. "I think there's time for a leisurely luncheon before the lady puts in her appearance."

I watched him head for the stairway to the Spartan Grill. . . .

At two thirty-five that afternoon Mr. Atterbury received a phone call from Kennedy Airport. It was Helwig, the Baroness' steward. They were, Helwig said, through customs and they would arrrive at the hotel in about a half an hour. Helwig trusted that all would be ready for them. All would, Atterbury assured him.

I was notified and I went down from my fourth-floor office to the lobby, leaving behind me a protesting Shelda.

"Someone has to mind the store," I told her.

The luncheon crowd had pretty well gone back to its offices on Fifth and Madison when I got downstairs. The lobby was relatively quiet. There were, however, two rather interesting observers occupying two of the big overstuffed armchairs. Sam Culver was working on a pipe with a little pocket tool. The man named Stephen Wood was several chairs away from Sam, chain-smoking cigarettes. A waiter had brought him a whiskey on the rocks. I saw him toss half of it down in one swallow. His black eyes were fixed on the main entrance, and they looked hot and hungry.

I walked over to Sam. "On the level, what's with your friend Wood?" I asked him.

Sam glanced at the dark man. "I'd say he's been pouring it on," he said. "Must have had half a dozen whiskies since we last saw him."

"Is he going to make some kind of trouble?"

"Too bad," Sam said. "It's your job to prevent it, isn't it?"

"Sam, Chambrun's your friend," I said.

He sighed. "I've been indulging myself in small-boy mystifying. I don't think he'll make any public trouble," he said. "I think he just wants Charmian to see him."

"And then what happens?"

"Presumably Charmian's blood starts to run cold," Sam said.

Just then I saw Jerry Dodd across the lobby. He's a thin, wiry little man in his late forties, with a professional smile that doesn't hide the fact that his pale, restless eyes are always searching for a sign of anything inimicable to the Beaumont's best interests. Chambrun trusts him without reservations, and his performance over the years as security officer has justified that trust. He's a shrewd, tough, yet tactful operator.

"It seems the staff is of the opinion the Baroness will do a strip tease as she comes in the revolving door," he said when I joined him. I noticed that a great many staff people seemed to have found business in the lobby.

"You know the guy in the corner chair—name of Stephen Wood?" I asked.

Jerry looked. "New to me," he said.

"Sam's hinting around he might try to make trouble for the lady," I said.

"Thanks for the tip," Jerry said, and moved casually toward the staring Mr. Wood.

At that moment the cavalcade from Kennedy arrived at the front entrance.

There were three large, magnificent-looking, air-conditioned Cadillacs. Two of them carried people and the third a collection of luggage that might have been manufactured in the mint. Waters, the Beaumont's elegant doorman, reached for the rear door of the first Cadillac, which obviously carried the queen. He was fast, but not fast enough. The door opened and out popped a man whom I identified from the newspaper clippings as John Masters, the bodyguard. He was slim, hard-faced, wearing a tightly belted trench coat, black glasses, and a black hat with the brim pulled down over his eyes. His hands were in his pockets and I visualized hair-trigger guns. He was right out of *The Man from U.N.C.L.E.*—pure camp.

Masters looked quickly up and down the street, satisfied himself that Fifth Avenue was devoid of assassins, and gave a brisk nod to the occupants of the car.

Out came another man, tall, square-shouldered, wearing a black Chesterfield with a velvet collar. He also wore black glasses, and gray hair showed under the rim of his black fedora, brim jerked downward. Helwig and Masters stood on each side of the open car door. The third passenger, however, did not appear.

The second Cadillac, instead, started to disgorge. Out came a short, obese little man, black-coated, hatted, and glassed like the others. He carried a small, black medical bag. This was Dr. Malinkov, "physician in residence." He moved, uncertainly, toward the revolving doors. He was followed by two women: a blond Amazon in her early fifties wearing a tweed coat with a mink collar and a little mink toque on her ash-blond hair; and a small, very pretty girl, also blond, carrying a black miniature poodle who yipped disapprovingly at Waters.

The two women and the three men now made a sort of alley between the first Cadillac and the door. Out of the car stepped another man, also wearing black glasses. But there the black motif ended. He was hatless, and his red hair was long, mod-style. He wore a double-breasted overcoat of pale-blue tweed with a heavy fur collar that looked like what I think sable looks like. The bottoms of his trousers were tight-fitting and, so help me, bright red. His shoes were a matching red in suede. He turned and held out his hand to the last passenger in the Cadillac.

The Baroness made her appearance, controlled but brisk. Her coat was black sable, her hat black sable. The coat was a three-quarter-length affair, and all that was visible below it was a pair of very shapely legs covered by sheer stockings that were, in effect, invisible. Her skirt was obviously fashionably short. One gloved hand held the coat together tightly at her throat. The other hand just touched the gigolo's fingers as she came out of the car and moved, quick and lithe, across the sidewalk. Helwig, the gray-haired man, wheeled in front of her, and Masters, the bodyguard, moved in directly behind her. It was as if it had been rehearsed many times. The girl with the pet poodle and the gigolo, Peter Wynn, came next. The Amazon and the doctor brought up the rear.

Did I mention that Charmian Zetterstrom also wore black glasses? The lights from the lobby chandeliers made them glitter as she came through the revolving door and started for the desk. She looked around, cool, self-possessed. She moved with the grace of a professional dancer. She suggested youth and a controlled vitality that were extraordinary for a woman of what I knew her age to be.

The whole campy entrance was ludicrous but I found my impulse to laugh choked off abruptly in my throat. Charmian Zetterstrom's hidden glance rested on me for a moment, held on me steadily. A cold wind ran along my spine. I felt like a helpless insect about to be pinned to a collector's card.

Then she looked away, and I realized my hands had been clenched so tightly that my fingers hurt.

Helwig was at the desk, talking to Mr. Atterbury.

Charmian Zetterstrom stood a few feet away, surveying the lobby with an air that wouldn't have pleased Chambrun. She gave the impression that the Beaumont looked pretty run-down to her.

Johnny Thacker, the day bell captain, and half a dozen bellhops came staggering through the revolving door with the gaudy luggage from the third Cadillac.

And then it happened. Stephen Wood was standing face to face with Charmian Zetterstrom.

"Charmian!" he said. His voice cracked like a pistol shot.

She looked at him, apparently completely undisturbed. If the sight of him made her blood run cold, as Sam Culver had predicted it might, there was no way to tell. And there was no time for a second reaction from her.

Masters, the bodyguard, acted so swiftly I couldn't really follow his moves. The back of his right hand seemed to catch Wood on the Adam's apple, like an axe blade. There was a gurgling cry from Wood as he tottered backwards. Masters' left hand, a triphammer, then caught him on the point of the jaw and Wood went over in something approximating a back somersault, and lay still. Masters was instantly standing over him, waiting for him to move, which he didn't.

Jerry Dodd, caught off base for one of the few times in his career, gave Masters a shove which wasn't expected and sent him staggering a few steps away from the prostrate Wood. Instantly there was a gun in Masters' hand, pointed straight at Jerry. Somebody screamed. I think it was the girl with the pet poodle.

"Put that away and get your whole goddamned army out of here," a cold voice said.

I turned to look at Chambrun, who was walking straight toward the gun, placing himself squarely between Masters and Jerry Dodd. I tried to move, and felt as if I had on diver's boots. It was Masters who wavered, not Chambrun. The bodyguard slowly lowered his gun and dropped it back in the pocket of his trench coat.

Charmian Zetterstrom was at Chambrun's elbow. "I apologize for Masters," she said, her voice as cool and clear as brook water. "I have been in some danger recently and he was only doing his job. You are Mr. Chambrun?"

Chambrun turned. "I am Pierre Chambrun."

"George Battle has spoken of you with the utmost regard."

"And he engages me to run this hotel, Baroness. I will not have this kind of horseplay." He looked over to where Johnny Thacker and two of his boys were helping Stephen Wood to his feet. The man's eyes were glazed, and a little trickle of blood ran from one corner of his slack mouth. "You know this man?"

"I've never seen him before in my life," Charmian Zetterstrom said, looking steadily at Wood. "His approach was so sudden, so startling, that Masters did the only thing he could do. You will concede, Mr. Chambrun, that a bodyguard can't wait until after an attack is made to go into action. It couldn't matter less what happens after it's too late. You do agree, don't you?"

Helwig, his face expressionless, his eyes hidden by the black glasses, moved in. "Your rooms are on the nineteenth floor, Baroness. They are ready." Chambrun might not have been there so far as Helwig was concerned. He signaled to the bellhops, the gigolo, the doctor, the Amazon, and the poodle carrier. They all started toward the elevators.

Charmian Zetterstrom gave Chambrun a bright, questioning smile. "With your permission, Mr. Chambrun?"

"No more gun-wavings," he said. "No more strong-arm stuff."

"Unless it is absolutely necessary," she said. She turned toward the elevators, and came face to face with Sam Culver. He was smiling too, his slow, gentle smile. She walked straight past him as though he were part of the lobby furniture. So much for having grown up with the lady in her pigtail days.

"Now that," Sam said to me, softly, "is the way to play a poker hand when you don't hold any cards."

2

Jerry Dodd and Frank Williams, one of the assistant house managers, helped a still tottering Stephen Wood to the hotel infirmary, which is on the lobby floor just behind the reception desk. The day nurse, Miss Kramer, sat Wood down in a chair and proceeded to clean up his bloody mouth and chin while a call went out for Dr. Partridge, the house physician. Miss Kramer is one of those jolly professionals who insists on asking, "How are we feeling?" or "Would we like a pillow back of our head?" She's in the infirmary all day with very little to do except, perhaps, to help someone get a chunk of soot out of an eye, or bandage a cut finger for a busboy who's handled a steak knife injudiciously. When she has anything that looks remotely like a real case she becomes slightly more than intolerable. Wood squirmed under the touch of her square, capable fingers. He was having difficulty talking. Evidently that vicious blow at his throat had temporarily paralyzed his vocal equipment.

Chambrun appeared on the scene before Dr. Partridge could be pried away from his backgammon game in the Spartan Bar.

"You've gotten his name?" he asked Jerry Dodd.

"He's having difficulty speaking," Jerry said.

"His name is Stephen Wood," I said.

"How do you know?" Chambrun asked.

"Sam Culver knows him."

"Is he registered here?"

I picked up a telephone and called Atterbury at the front desk. Stephen Wood was not a guest of the Beaumont.

"Mr. Wood," Chambrun said, "do you w~nt to bring assault charges against the Baroness' bodyguard?"

Wood shook his head, slowly, from side to side.

"What were your intentions when you confronted the Baroness?"

Wood just stared straight ahead.

"He's not armed," Jerry Dodd said. Jerry hadn't made any sort of formal search, but in the process of getting Wood to his feet and helping him to the infirmary he'd evidently made certain there were no weapons hidden under the tweed jacket.

"What was your purpose?" Chambrun asked again. His voice wasn't friendly.

Wood moistened his lips. His voice, when he tried it, was a husky whisper. "I—I made a mistake," he said.

"Mistake?"

"She—she isn't the woman I thought she was."

"You called her by her first name," I said.

"It was a mistake," Wood said, his eyes lowered.

"It is a little difficult to mistake the Baroness for someone else," Chambrun said.

Wood swallowed painfully. "Nonetheless," he said.

"Who did you think she was?" Chambrun asked.

"Someone else," Wood said.

"Someone else named Charmian?" Chambrun asked.

"I tell you it was a mistake," Wood said. "I thought she was someone else."

"Someone else named Charmian?"

"For Godsake, how many times do I have to tell you it was a mistake? Please, I'd like to get out of here."

"Not till Dr. Partridge has checked you out," Chambrun said. "We have possible lawsuits to consider. What is your address, Mr. Wood?"

Wood muttered the name of a flea-bag hotel on the West Side. "There'll be no lawsuits."

At that moment Doc Partridge came in, grumbling. The dice had been rolling well for him for a change and he resented being called away from a winning streak.

"I want a full report on what you find," Chambrun said. He turned for the door, giving me a little nod that indicated he wanted me to go with him. Out in the lobby he turned to me, exasperated.

"What do you make of that double talk?"

"It was no mistake," I said. I gave him a brief account of my conversation about Wood with Sam, and how Wood had been waiting in the lobby for Charmian Zetterstrom's arrival.

"Tell Sam Culver I want to see him in my office," Chambrun said, and started away. He was stopped by a signal from Atterbury at the desk. We walked over. Atterbury was smiling his sphinxlike smile.

"You are summoned into the Presence," he said to Chambrun.

"Be good enough to speak English," Chambrun said.

"You are to wait upon the Baroness at your earliest convenience. I quote. Helwig, the steward, just phoned down. Maybe she doesn't like the wallpaper in 19-B."

Chambrun looked at me. "See what she wants. And get me Sam Culver." He walked briskly away.

Atterbury grinned at me. "Watch your step," he said. "I understand she eats attractive young men alive." . . .

No two suites at the Beaumont look alike. Floor plans are much the same, but each one has been individually decorated to give it its own character. 19-B is a gem of eighteenth-century French delicacies. It is strictly designed to satisfy female taste; the four rooms are in different pastel shades, with gold the basic furniture color. The paintings on the walls are not reproductions, but who the artists were only Chambrun knows. A woman was supposed to squeal with delight when she first walked in. There was a huge double bed in one of the bedrooms, a single in the other. There was a small, very modern kitchenette.

I was admitted to the suite by the blond poodle carrier after I had explained that Chambrun wasn't available at the moment and that I was his deputy. The girl seemed doubtful until Charmian Zetterstrom's clear, cool voice came to us from the living room.

"Ask Mr. Haskell to come in, Heidi."

She sat on a gold-brocade-covered love seat, facing me as I walked in. The black glasses were gone, and she had the bluest blue eyes I can ever remember seeing. She had on a simple pale-yellow shift that ended several inches above very shapely knees. The lovely legs were tucked up under her on the love seat.

She was, I told myself, something of a miracle. She had married Conrad Zetterstrom twenty years ago. She had to be close to forty. Without the facts you couldn't have believed it. The dark hair had the sheen of a bird's wing. That can be managed in a beauty shop. The yellow shift was high-necked, but her arms were bare. I looked for a little forty-year-old flabbiness near the armpits. There was none. I looked for the lines around those magical blue eyes and on the slender neck that Shelda had promised me would be there. They were nonexistent. If there was anything tell-tale at all, it was that the pale skin was obviously overlaid, skillfully, with some sort of pancake makeup. It had the texture of an actor's face, which has been cold-creamed each night and twice on matinee days. Her body looked firm, and young, and exciting. The Amazon masseuse must be a genius, I thought.

"Come in, Mr. Haskell," she said. "Please sit down." She

27

gestured toward a frail-looking armchair next to the love seat. "Can I have Heidi get you a drink?"

She was apparently completely organized after less than half an hour in her new quarters.

I sat, feeling a little as though I'd been called on the carpet by my fourth-grade schoolteacher. I had, I may say in passing, been madly in love with that fourth-grade teacher. I declined the drink.

"You are Mr. Chambrun's assistant?" she asked.

"I'm the hotel's public relations director," I said, "which means that I am also its number-one trouble shooter. There's something that displeases you?"

"On the contrary, I couldn't be more delighted with the arrangements you've made for us."

For some idiotic reason I remembered Atterbury's remark about musical beds. "How can I help you?" I asked.

"I want to give a party," she said. "Except for a short stay in London this is the first time I've been off Zetterstrom Island in twenty years. I want to—how do you say?—do it up brown."

"Fine," I said. "Parties are our business. Anything from coming out balls to intimate dinners in a private dining room."

"I have something modest as to numbers in mind," she said. "Say fifty to seventy-five people." She leaned back a little, blue-shaded eyelids half lowered. "I want an *apéritif* such as no one has ever drunk before. I want hors d'oeuvres such as no one has ever seen or tasted before. I want a dinner that will make the world's gourmets concede it tops anything they've ever feasted on before. I want wines from strange, exotic places that go down like liquid gold. I want music that will make the guests swoon with delight." The eyelids rose and the blue eyes fastened on me. "Can you arrange all that, Mr. Haskell?"

"Mr. Amato, our banquet manager, is your man. He will jump up and down with pleasure at the prospect of planning a dinner on which there is no cost limit. I assume there is no limit."

"None."

"Let me talk to him. When he's had a chance to formulate some suggestions I'll arrange for him to come to see you. How soon do you want to give this dinner?"

Her eyes were very bright. "I'm like a child giving a first birthday party. I wish it could be tomorrow. But I know it's impossible. I want it as soon as your Mr. Amato can arrange for all the things I've requested."

"It shouldn't take too much time," I said. "Amato knows exactly where to go for the most unusual rarities."

"There is one other thing," she said. "The guest list."

"Oh?"

"I have been what you might call a recluse all these years. I have very few friends."

"Fifty to seventy-five are more than most people have," I said.

"Oh, but I haven't anything like that number of friends," she said. "Three or four at the outside that I know are in New York. I particularly want to have a man named Samuel Culver. He is the only must."

"Sam may not be very pleased with you at the moment," I said. "You cut him dead in the lobby a little while back."

The blue eyes widened, and I thought I saw a slight nerve-twitch high up on a lacquered cheek. "He was there?"

"Inches away from you," I said.

"Oh, my God!" she said. Then: "It must have been the excitement. I was so eager to get away from the trouble Masters had caused—if you see Sam, will you explain?"

"Sure," I said. "He probably understood. He's an understanding-type guy."

"Don't I know it?" she said.

"Does Stephen Wood go on your guest list?"

"Who is Stephen Wood?"

"The man your Masters slugged in the lobby."

"Of course not. He's a complete stranger."

"So let's get back to the guest list," I said.

She smiled at me. "You are to supply the guests," she said.

I just stared at her.

"Surely there must be hundreds of fascinating people in the worlds of art, music, science, politics, theatre, who would be intrigued at the prospect of a fabulous dinner and an opportunity to meet the much-talked-about and mysterious Baroness Zetterstrom."

"Well, yes, but—"

"I leave the guest list to you, Mr. Haskell."

I felt tongue-tied. "Shall I convey an invitation to Sam

Culver?"

"Please, no," she said. "I'd like to do that myself. But if you will explain to him how I happened not to see him in the lobby, and ask him if he'd come to see me, I'd be grateful."

"My pleasure," I said.

A relaxed smile lit up her strangely lovely face. "Since we will be involved closely with the details for the party, Mr. Haskell, can we stop being formal? What is your first name?"

"Mark."

"May I call you Mark? And you will call me Charmian. So that's settled." She sounded as though she'd just decided on the precise hour for D day. "You may tell Mr. Chambrun that I am altogether delighted with his emissary, and that he needn't make the effort to apportion any of his valuable time to me."

She held out her hand, and I think I was expected to kiss it, Continental fashion. I wasn't up to that. I just touched her fingers with mine and gave her a half-comic little bow. At the same moment I felt as if a mild charge of electricity had gone through me. . . .

Sam Culver lives at the Beaumont. He owns one of the smallest cooperative units in the upper regions of the hotel, a comfortable living room, small bedroom and bath, and a tiny kitchenette. The living room, except for casement windows looking out over the East River and the 59th Street bridge, is walled-in by books. The furniture is heavy and comfortable. Sam does quite a bit of traveling and often the small apartment stands empty. Maintaining this *pied-à-terre* is the only indication in Sam's way of life that he is anything more than very modestly well-off.

When Sam was reached with the message that Chambrun wanted to see him in his office, he called Chambrun on the house phone and suggested that they get together in Sam's apartment.

"I think I know what you want to see me about, Pierre. Wouldn't there be less chance of interruption up here? It's not a simple story."

And so, while I was being subjected to the special charms of the Baroness Zetterstrom, the mountain went to Mohammed.

When Chambrun was settled comfortably in a deep armchair, a Dubonnet on the rocks—the strongest drink he ever takes during working hours—on a side table by the chair, Sam began to talk, filling a pipe from a variety of tobacco tins on his desk.

"Mark has told you, Pierre, that I said Stephen Wood might turn Charmian Zetterstrom's blood cold when he confronted her. It didn't happen. Either she didn't know him or she has at last become the greatest actress in the world."

Chambrun flicked the ash from his Egyptian cigarette into a silver ashtray next to his drink. Sam was holding a lighter to his pipe.

"You know Wood and some history that connects him with the Baroness?" Chambrun asked. "She ignored him, says he is a complete stranger; he says he made a mistake. She is not, he says, the woman he thought she was."

Sam puffed blue clouds. "You know me, Pierre, on the subject of surface facts versus subsurface truths. The surface facts may be a little puzzling to you. I think it's true that Charmian never laid eyes on Stephen Wood before. I think it may also be truth of a sort when Wood says Charmian isn't the woman he thought she was." Sam grinned at Chambrun. "You think of me, I imagine, as a reasonably sober, well-oriented, unneurotic, fundamentally moral person. If you were to discover that I was, in fact, the Boston Strangler, you might say, 'He's not the man I thought he was.' Wood was speaking that way, I think. He wasn't mistaken in thinking she was Charmian Zetterstrom. But when she didn't react at the sight of him he concluded she was not the woman he'd thought she was."

"Which in plain English means——?"

"Stephen Wood is a German Jew by birth," Sam said. "His name originally was Wald, German for 'wood.' Ten years ago his twin brother, Bruno Wald, was perhaps the top romantic leading man in German films. You have to realize, Pierre, that over here the Zetterstroms and Zetterstrom Island had never been heard of by more than a couple of dozen people. In Europe they were famous. There was endless talk about the wild parties, the incredible luxury, the debaucheries. Everybody and his brother in the upper echelons of society and the arts, and the simply rich, tried to wangle invitations to the Island. They were few and far between, and the people who did get there came back curiously silent about what had actually gone on. Perhaps because they hoped to be reinvited; perhaps because they couldn't risk talking lest they themselves be talked about. This enhanced the mystery of the place, and made the uninvited all the more eager.

"If you can imagine Stephen Wood with more flesh and muscle on his bones, his dark eyes laughing and not tortured, the grim lines of personal agony erased from his face, you might have a picture of his brother, Bruno Wald. The Wald brothers were identical twins at birth. But they became easily identifiable as they grew to manhood. Bruno was bold, dashing, high-spirited; Stephen was dark, brooding, almost satanic. Well, ten years ago Bruno found himself the recipient of an invitation to Zetterstrom Island. He accepted with delight. He was flown from Athens to the Island in Zetterstrom's private plane. A week or so later Stephen received a telephone call from Marcus Helwig, the Zetterstroms' steward, or manager, or whatever he calls himself. He was sorry to report that Bruno Wald had been lost at sea in a yachting accident. He had drowned. His body had not been recovered.

"There was a three-day excitement in the German press. Bruno was, after all, a popular matinee idol. There was also an opportunity for much gossip about the notorious Zetterstroms. But the Greek authorities who investigated as a routine matter found no reason to doubt the story. There had been a storm at sea—I suspect a small hurricane. Several fishing boats had been lost on the same day.

"I should say here that Stephen had no reason to doubt

34

the story either. He attended a memorial service for his brother in West Berlin and then he came to the United States. He's an electronics engineer and he had been offered a very good job with a firm here in New York. Whenever he was introduced as Stephen Wald he was suddenly recognized as a sort of double of his late brother. To avoid the endless talk and gossip about Bruno he changed his name to Wood.

"The tragedy of Bruno Wald's death was long forgotten by the public. Stephen, I think, despite the close tie with a twin, had managed to throw it off and involve himself totally in a new life. Then one evening, ten years after Bruno's death, Stephen came home to find the wreckage of what had once been Bruno, waiting for him on his doorstep. Bruno was very much not dead."

"You're going a little fast for me," Chambrun said. "Bruno was not dead. Why hadn't he communicated with Stephen?"

"That is the nub of the story," Sam said. He looked at his pipe, which had gone out. He hesitated and then put it down, regretfully, on his desk. "It was almost simply instinct that made Bruno recognizable to Stephen. He was skin and bones. His face was lined, the color of ashes. He wore old, stained clothes that looked as though they'd come out of a rummage sale. Bruno had always been a great dandy. When Stephen spoke to him, recognized him, Bruno burst into tears, like a frightened child. He needed Stephen's help to struggle down the inner hall to Stephen's apartment. Inside, he collapsed on a sofa, weeping.

"You can imagine the questions that poured out of Stephen. What in God's name had happened to him? Why hadn't he been in touch? The answers finally came choking out of Bruno. There had been no yachting accident. He had arrived at Zetterstrom Island that day ten years ago for his long weekend visit. He didn't take time to describe the old Baron's Shangri-La, but his shaken voice implied that everything about it was now loathsome to him. He had been there only a few hours when the beautiful and glamorous Charmian made it quite clear to him that she was his for the asking. Bruno had, quite frankly, gone there anticipating some sort of exotic experience. Charmian, evidently, was to be it.

"Bruno was incapable of describing to his brother that experience as it must have been. But making love to Charmian had evidently surpassed anything he had ever thought of in erotic imaginings. There were no other guests on the Island that weekend. For three or four days Bruno was totally involved with the lady. He was young in those days and he could satisfy all her requirements. But presently, despite the wild excitement of this love affair, carried on quite openly under the eyes of the old Baron and the elaborate staff of people, the time came when Bruno had to get back to West Berlin to meet a film commitment. It was then that the old Baron called him into his study. He asked Bruno how much money he was making in films, and then offered to double it if Bruno would stay on the Island. Charmian wanted him as a permanent possession.

"Bruno thought the old man was kidding, but he wasn't. The whole situation was suddenly revolting to Bruno. He refused, politely, and asked when he could be flown back to Athens. The Baron then made the position quite clear. Bruno was not going to be flown back to Athens. If Charmian wanted him, Charmian was going to have him. He was a prisoner. Bruno thought it was a miserable joke, and then he found out it was very much not a joke. Charmian had been prepared to buy him, and if he couldn't be bought she would keep him anyway.

"A few days later there was actually a storm at sea. That was when word was sent back to the mainland that Bruno had died in a yachting accident. The whole situation was unbelievable. There were no telephones to the mainland, no way Bruno could manage to communicate. He told himself that if he continued his relationship with Charmian for a few days she would tire of him and the whole ghastly situation would resolve itself. But presently he realized that it didn't matter whether she tired of him or not. He became aware of other people on the island for the first time. He recognized some of them. The Baron's island was being used as a haven for some of the most wanted German war criminals. Knowing this he was lost. He realized they would never let him go back to the world again. But she didn't tire of him. He began to be torn to pieces by a terrible panic. It was for real. He began to try to plan some sort of escape. There was the plane, and Bruno was a licensed pilot. There were half a dozen powerboats. He was very cagey about it. He watched the comings and goings carefully. His idea was that he would steal one of the powerboats. He decided he would select one that had been recently used, so there'd be no question of a cold motor. He picked his moment, after dark, and raced for the boathouse. He chose the launch he'd been watching, its engine still warm to the touch. His finger was on the starter button when John Masters, the lady's bodyguard, whom you saw in the lobby, rose up out of the cockpit, grinning.

" 'We'll always be miles ahead of you, Mr. Wald,' Masters said. 'So go back to the house and tend to your knitting.'

"That's the way it was, not for a few days or weeks but year after year. He could no longer make love to the lady. The sight of her made him retch. But in spite of this he was kept there, brought into her presence every day, pawed, insulted, on occasion actually stripped and flogged in her presence by one of the menservants. This seemed to provide her with some sort of erotic excitement."

"Ten years of this?" Chambrun asked, in a low, hard voice.

"So Bruno told Stephen that day in New York. Toward the end Bruno came down with some illness. Dr. Malinkov took care of him, but was noncommittal. Whatever it was, Bruno began to waste away physically. The lady seemed to lose interest in torturing him. The guard against escape seemed to relax a little. Bruno wasn't capable of any great physical effort. But one night he made it, in, of all things, a rowboat. There was no moon and the sea was angry.

Still, he struggled away from the Island, pulling on the oars with hands that began to bleed. He knew they would come after him. They wouldn't dare let him get back to the mainland to tell his story. He knew what he would do if he heard one of the powerboats coming toward him through the night. There was a fisherman's knife on the rear seat of the rowboat. He would take it, systematically cut his throat with it, and slip over the side into the cool death of the sea. He was dizzy with exhaustion when a big wave hit the little boat broadside and capsized it. Bruno managed to cling to the overturned boat, consciousness slowly slipping away from him. He blacked out.

"When he came to, he was lying in a bunk in the hold of an evil-smelling ship of some sort. He'd been picked up by a Greek freighter which was on its way to the United States. Bruno thought they must be carrying narcotics of some sort, because they were making no interim stops before New York. They refused to let him use the ship's radio. They didn't treat him badly, fed him whatever there was to eat. Bruno lay for days on his bunk in the hold, alternately sweating and freezing. There was no ship's doctor, and whatever his illness was it was slowly destroying him.

"Then, that afternoon, the ship docked in New York and no one stopped Bruno from going ashore. He called an old family friend and asked for Stephen's whereabouts. He didn't identify himself because the one thing in the world he wanted was to keep word from getting back to the Zetterstroms. They would certainly come after him.

He knew too much about them and their wanted friends. That was Bruno's story."

"Not pretty," Chambrun said.

Sam picked up his pipe and relit it. "Stephen's first thought was to get a doctor for Bruno. He was suddenly seized with melodramatic panics of his own. Bruno's story, his presence here, must be kept secret. A doctor he knew had an office down the block—a very busy office. The doctor would take forever if Stephen tried to impress him with the urgency of the situation on the phone. The doctor's nurse might listen to the story on an extension. So Stephen made his brother comfortable and set off on foot, running for the doctor's office. It took, at the most, fifteen minutes for Stephen to get in to see the doctor, explain, and bring him back, both running to the apartment.

"Bruno was in the bathroom. He was dead. He had apparently cut his throat with one of Stephen's razor blades."

Chambrun's eyes widened. "Apparently?"

"The apartment door was open when Stephen and the doctor came back. Stephen was almost sure he'd locked it when he went out. He convinced himself that someone from the Zetterstroms had been that close on Bruno's heels."

"And the police?"

"They listened, politely, to what was obviously an Arabian Nights' nightmare. An autopsy showed that Bruno had a malignant tumor, very close to the brain. It could have affected his rationality. There was no Greek freighter moored at a North River pier. There had been one, to be sure, but it had docked only long enough to unload a very small cargo. Radio communication with the captain had negative results. They had picked no one up in the Mediterranean; they had brought no passenger to New York. Stephen found a reasonably patient Homicide detective, who admitted that it was odd there were no fingerprints on the razor blade, Bruno's or any other's. He started a laborious inquiry with the Greek authorities, reopening the story of the yachting accident, then ten years back. There seemed to be no question about it. There were half a dozen witnesses to Bruno's having been swept overboard in the storm. Zetterstrom people, of course. The equivalent of our Coast Guard had searched for the body for many days. They had gone pretty thoroughly over the battered yacht and Zetterstrom Island itself. Naturally there had been ample time for them to get their wanted war criminals to another place of safety. The police were convinced.

"But Bruno was dead in Stephen's bathroom and he had certainly been alive all those years. But where? There was finally a large, official shrug in both New York and Athens. Obviously Bruno had survived the storm. Probably he'd been badly injured. They suggested a blow on the head which had finally led to the growth of the tumor, which would certainly have been fatal in a few weeks, had Bruno lived. The suggestion was a prolonged amnesia. He could have been wandering all those years somewhere in Africa or the Middle East, a man without identity. Stephen kept insisting that even if Bruno had lost his memory, there were thousands of people who would instantly have recognized him as a famous movie star. True, the authorities admitted, but it hadn't happened. War criminals? They were constantly being reported seen all over the world—South America, Asia, Africa. They were certainly not on Zetterstrom Island. The case was closed."

"But not for Stephen Wood," Chambrun said.

"No, not for Stephen," Sam said. "He was like the Ancient Mariner, telling his story to anyone who would listen. I was one of the people he buttonholed at a party somewhere. Being what I am, I was interested. It was a colossal story if it was true. But I've never been able to find one shred of evidence that proves the whole thing wasn't some last-ditch delirium of Bruno's. But today I thought I might find out."

"The confrontation in the lobby," Chambrun said.

Sam nodded. "Suppose it was true—Bruno's story. Charmian arrives at the hotel and is suddenly confronted by Bruno in the flesh—actually his twin, but to her he must almost certainly be a stunning shock. I think Stephen counted on that. She would betray herself when she found herself suddenly face to face with someone who must seem to be Bruno."

"But nothing happened. God, she was an iceberg."

Sam nodded, frowning. "I know. Could she have been so controlled when she was unexpectedly faced by a man she had loved, tortured, and destroyed for years? Could she be that good an actress—not a flicker of an eyelid? I think she convinced Stephen. She couldn't have faced him so blankly, without emotion, if there was even a small portion of truth to Bruno's story. That's what he meant, I think, when he said she wasn't the woman he thought she was. The woman Bruno had described to him couldn't have survived that confrontation without some small, revealing reaction."

"Stephen may no longer look like Bruno," Chambrun said.

"Very much like him," Sam said. "Only the normal changes that take place in ten years." He shook his head slowly. "That's the most extraordinary part of the whole thing. Charmian hasn't changed, physically, in twenty years. Not by so much as a misplaced hair. She is exactly as I last saw her, only a few months before she married Conrad Zetterstrom. It's impossible and yet it's so."

"The modern beautician can work miracles," Chambrun said. "She evidently carried one with her—the Amazon." His bright eyes narrowed. "She didn't seem to know you, and I gather from Mark that you're an old friend. She didn't react to you either."

Sam's smile was enigmatic. "That's something else again," he said. "I don't think the lady likes me. I was being deliberately snubbed."

Chambrun pulled himself up out of his chair. "As a hotel manager I'm concerned about one thing. How crazy is Stephen Wood? Am I to expect more melodrama from him?"

"Hard to say," Sam said. "If he's convinced, no. If, after

he thinks about it, he isn't convinced, yes."

Sam's front doorbell rang. It was me, fresh from my visit with the electric Charmian.

"Ruysdale told me you were both here," I said, when Sam let me in. Miss Ruysdale is Chambrun's incomparable private secretary. "I have a message for you, Sam. From Charmian."

"She was always quick on the first name stuff," he said, his smile wry.

"She didn't see you in the lobby. She was disturbed by what had happened. She conveys a thousand apologies and wants you to come and see her."

"Well, well," Sam said.

"She's giving a dinner party for you," I said, enjoying myself. Sam just stared at me. I gave them both a quick outline of my interview with the lady.

"It sounds like her," Sam said. "Whatever she wants she assumes she can have—including people." He glanced at Chambrun.

"Never put off till tomorrow etcetera, etcetera," Chambrun said.

Sam nodded. He picked up the phone on his desk. "Please connect me with the Baroness Zetterstrom's suite," he said.

None of us knew that at that precise moment the hallman on the nineteenth floor was staring with disbelief at the mangled remains of a small French poodle which had been stuffed into a trash can near the service elevator.

3

Young Mr. Peter Wynn, referred to in these early pages as "the gigolo," created something of a sensation when he appeared in the Trapeze Bar shortly before six o'clock that evening. His long red hair, carefully set, his red trousers and red suede shoes, his pale-blue Edwardian frock coat with a ruffled white shirt showing at neck and cuffs provided the extreme in Carnaby Street styling. He must have been aware that everyone in the place was suddenly staring at him, including Shelda and me from our corner table, but he was completely imperturable as he perched on a bar stool and asked for a champagne cocktail. He mentioned a vintage year that provided him with a glimmer of respect from Eddie, the bartender.

The Trapeze Bar is suspended in space, like a bird-cage, over the foyer to the Beaumont's grand ballroom. The Trapeze, its walls an elaborate Florentine grillwork, is popular mainly because it's different. An artist of the

Calder school has decorated it with mobiles of circus performers working on trapezes. They sway slightly in the gentle draft from a concealed air-cooling system. It is a predinner meeting place for the very rich, the very elegant, and the very notorious. It is presided over by one Mr. DelGreco, who, like all the maître d's and captains at the Beaumont, is suave, a master of the art of supplying real service, and a shrewd student of human nature. He is also kept informed, like all the others, as to exactly who's who on the Beaumont's list of guests.

Mr. DelGreco was suddenly at young Mr. Wynn's elbow, holding a lighter for a cigarette which the young man had produced from a silver cigarette case.

"May I find a table for you, Mr. Wynn?" DelGreco asked, "or are you waiting for someone?"

The use of his name obviously surprised Wynn. I found myself repressing a giggle as I watched. Wynn was a little like Batman appearing at some formal party in Gotham City.

"As a matter of fact, I'm looking for a dog," Wynn said, "and I got thirsty. You haven't seen a small black poodle running around anywhere, have you?"

"Dogs are not allowed in the Trapeze Bar," DelGreco said.

"Oh, this dog doesn't pay any attention to signs," Wynn said. "The world is his oyster. His name is Puzzi. If you call him by name he may answer. If you see him, tell him the Baroness is very worried about him."

DelGreco's face was a mask. "I'll tell him," he said.

"Meanwhile, if the Baroness has lost her dog have you reported it to Mr. Dodd, our security officer?"

"The little man who pushes people around? I think I'd rather not," Wynn said. "What about Mr. Haskell, the public relations bird? Isn't that he over in the corner?"

"Would you like to talk to him?" DelGreco asked.

"I think I would," Wynn said, reaching for the champagne cocktail Eddie brought him. He sipped, and then blotted at his red lips with a lace-edged handkerchief which he produced from the sleeve of his blue frock coat.

DelGreco came over to where Shelda and I were sitting.

"The Baroness has lost her dog," DelGreco said. "The young man wants to talk to you about it."

"Ask him to join us," I said, "and tell Eddie to repeat whatever it is he's drinking."

"Champagne cocktail," DelGreco said.

I grinned at him. "It goes on my expense account," I said.

Shelda's hand closed over mine under the edge of the table. It was cold. "Do you suppose he—he's another prisoner?" she asked.

Chambrun had repeated the story of Bruno Wald to me and I, in turn, had passed it on to Shelda.

"If he is, the chains are invisible," I said.

DelGreco delivered my message and young Mr. Wynn waved to us across the room. He indicated his drink to DelGreco and the captain picked it up and followed Wynn toward our table. Every eye in the Trapeze Bar

47

followed his progress. Just as he reached the table a waiter produced a third chair. I introduced Shelda, and Wynn gave her a polite, formal bow. Close up he looked just a little older than I'd supposed he was. No longer in his twenties, there were the beginnings of what would be lines of character in his face. It was hard to tell yet whether they could be weak or strong. His eyes were a cold, pale blue and unexpectedly shrewd, but he played the part of a foppish clown.

"It's Puzzi," he said, giving us a half-comic little shrug.

"The poodle?"

"He seems to have slipped out of Charmian's suite and disappeared into thin air."

"He shouldn't be hard to find in the hotel," I said. I signaled to a waiter and asked him to bring a telephone to our table.

"Puzzi is a newish member of the family," Wynn said. "Charmian is mad for him. If anything has happened to him she'll probably sue your friend Chambrun for the gold fillings in his teeth."

I picked up the phone the waiter brought and had myself connected with Jerry Dodd in his office. I gave him instructions to organize a dog-hunt.

Shelda was watching Wynn with the kind of fascination that a snake charmer produces in a snake. I had to concede that he certainly gave off male vibrations in spite of his fancy dress.

"We're all a little stir-crazy," Wynn said, as he extracted a cigarette from his silver case after offering one to Shelda. "Charmian hasn't been off the Island for twenty years. Most of the rest of us have been there for varying lengths of time. Helwig and Masters have been there longer than Charmian. Getting out in the world is a little dizzy-making."

"You've been there a long time?" I asked.

Wynn's smile was tight and thin. "I went there for a weekend eighteen months ago," he said. "I was offered a job and I stayed. I'm new compared to the rest."

I felt Shelda's knee press against mine. It was a little like Bruno Wald's story, only obviously Peter Wynn had not found the job distasteful.

"I'm a weak character," he said, as though he'd read my mind. "I prefer luxury to accomplishment."

A waiter picked up his empty glass and produced the fresh drink I'd ordered.

"What is the Island like?" Shelda asked him. "One hears so much about it, and yet I've never heard anything that really describes it."

Wynn's eyelids lowered and he seemed to be looking past us at some distant place. "The climate is unbelievable," he said. "Always warm, the air heavy with the scent of exotic flowers. You lie in the sun, you dream of something you want; you turn your head and there it is."

"Like for instance?" Shelda asked.

The pale-blue eyes turned her way, and a thin smile moved his lips. "Like a beautiful woman," he said. And then, quickly: "Like a bunch of purple grapes; like a new suit of clothes; like a peacock on the lawn; like a dry, dry wine, properly iced; like a cheese made from the milk of celestial goats; like—like anything you can dream of."

"Like freedom?" Shelda asked, quietly.

Wynn laughed, and it was tinged with bitterness. "You are a shrewd cookie, Miss Mason," he said. He reached for his champagne cocktail.

DelGreco appeared at my elbow. "You are wanted on the second floor," he said, in a discreetly low voice. That meant Chambrun.

I made my apologies to the peacock fancier. Shelda started to rise to go with me.

"Please, Miss Mason, won't you stay and have one drink with me?" Wynn asked. "You are my first real contact in a very long time with the outside world. I find it heady stuff."

The jerk, I thought. You didn't have to be a prisoner on a distant island to find Shelda heady stuff. She gave me a small, questing smile. Obviously she was dying to get more information about the Zetterstroms.

"Stay, of course," I said. "Don't worry about Puzzi, Mr. Wynn. They'll collect him for you in no time."

I went down to the lobby and up to Chambrun's office. Miss Ruysdale was at her desk in the outer office. She looked as though she'd been recently ill.

If there is an indispensable member of Chambrun's staff it is Miss Betsy Ruysdale. She's not easy to describe. Chambrun has many requirements in a personal secretary: She must be efficient beyond any normal demand. She must be prepared eternally to anticipate his needs without waiting for orders. She must be prepared to forget anything resembling regular working hours. She must be chic but not disturbing; Chambrun doesn't want his staff members mooning over some glamorous doll in his outer office, but neither does he want to be offended by someone unattractive. By some miracle, Miss Ruysdale meets all these requirements. Her clothes are quiet, but smart and expensive. Her manner toward the staff is friendly, touched by a nice humor, but there is an invisible line drawn over which no one steps. She is clearly all woman, yet there is no obvious man in her life unless the rumor about Chambrun himself is true. Her devotion to him is obviously total, but questionably romantic. He neuters her by calling her Ruysdale—never Miss Ruysdale or Betsy.

"I trust you have a strong stomach this evening," Miss Ruysdale said to me.

"What's up?" I asked.

She waved toward Chambrun's elegant private office and I went in, wondering.

Chambrun was seated at his desk, wearing his stone face. Jerry Dodd was there and a man in a neat suit of blue coveralls whom I recognized as one of the maintenance crew. His name, it turned out, was Powalsky. On a chair near the door was a bundle wrapped in a white sheet which appeared to be bloodstained.

Chambrun's cold eyes flicked my way. He gestured toward the sheet. "Take a look," he said.

I went over to the chair and, gingerly, opened up the sheet to see what was in it. I nearly tossed my cookies on the spot. Someone had slaughtered a small black poodle. The head was crushed like an eggshell. The body looked as though it had been ripped and torn by what must have been a large but dull knife with a jagged edge. I quickly covered the remains of the dog and turned, knowing that I must be a shade of pale green.

"You found this an hour ago," Chambrun said, ice in his voice, "but you didn't report it until word went out to look for the dog?"

"Gee, Mr. Chambrun, I would have reported it at the end of my shift," Powalsky said. "But I mean, it was just a dog."

"Would you wait till the end of your shift to report a murder?" Chambrun asked.

"No, Mr. Chambrun, but—it was just a dog."

"It was a murder," Chambrun said, grimly.

Jerry Dodd was fumbling with a cigarette. "No sign of the knife anywhere," he said. "At least, not on the nineteenth floor or anywhere near the trash can where Powalsky found it."

Chambrun looked at Jerry. "No one has reported seeing or hearing anything?"

"We're checking," Jerry said.

"Maybe the whole staff thinks it was 'just a dog,'" Chambrun said, his eyes bleak. "The violence involved is incredible."

"The blow on the head must have come first," Jerry said, "or you'd have heard the poor little bastard screaming from here to Staten Island."

"Or Zetterstrom Island," Chambrun said. He stood up. "The Baroness will have to be told. I don't relish it. Would you like to come with me, Mark?"

"No, but I will," I said. . . .

The pretty little blond maid, Heidi, answered Chambrun's ring at the door of 19-B.

"I'm afraid the Baroness is occupied," she said to Chambrun.

"It's rather important," he said.

"I will see. Please wait."

We waited in the small foyer and could hear the sound of voices in the sitting room. Then the foyer door was reopened by Sam Culver, his face noncommittal.

"Come in, gents," he said.

Charmian was still wearing the pale-yellow shift she'd had on earlier and she was still sitting on the gold-brocade love seat.

"Mr. Chambrun," she said. "And Mark!" She made it sound as though I was real pleasure. "I've just been renewing an old friendship with Sam. We knew each other a long time ago." She must have sensed the nonsocial coldness in Chambrun's attitude. "What is it, Mr. Chambrun?"

"Your dog, Baroness."

"Puzzi! You've found him?"

"We've found him, brutally killed."

Red-enameled fingers flew to her mouth. The electric-blue eyes were suddenly wide as saucers.

"There is no way to tell it pleasantly," Chambrun said.

"Someone crushed in his head and then ripped him to pieces with some kind of knife. He was stuffed into a trash can in the service area only a few yards from your door."

She was on her feet, straight as a string. "Masters! Marcus!" she said, quietly.

Instantly the door at the far end of the room opened, and Masters, the bodyguard, and Helwig, the steward, appeared together. It was interesting to discover that everything that was said in this room was evidently being monitored by these trusties. Both of them still wore black glasses.

"You heard?" Charmian asked.

"Yes, madame," Helwig said.

"Find out who did it and—and—" She couldn't finish. She was trembling from head to foot. "Poor little Puzzi."

"I'll take care of whoever it was," Masters said. He was smiling, and his thin lips were moist.

"You'll do nothing of the sort," Chambrun said. "My staff and I will find the answers. Whoever is responsible will be dealt with properly."

"That's not good enough, Mr. Chambrun," Charmian said. "An eye for an eye! Whoever did it will be made to suffer just as Puzzi suffered."

"And it will be a pleasure," Masters said. He sounded hungry.

"Mr. Chambrun is right, of course," Helwig said, in a flat, emotionless voice.

Charmian turned her head to look at him. I had the sudden conviction that this hard-faced, gray-haired man was the boss of the outfit. Charmian looked away from him.

"I'm sorry, Mr. Chambrun," she said. "I guess I lost my head. Of course it's your job. But my anger—when you told me—"

I looked at Masters. His smile was white and fixed. I had the feeling he wasn't listening.

"The Baroness will deeply appreciate your efforts to find the person responsible for this piece of villainy," Helwig said. "It's hard to believe anyone could behave so viciously toward a small dog. It's an act that shouldn't go unpunished—but legally, of course."

I saw that Chambrun hadn't missed the note of cool authority in Helwig's voice. "I'd like to ask the Baroness a question," he said, with a touch of irony that suggested he was asking Helwig's permission.

Helwig nodded, as though the request were quite normal.

"You say you didn't recognize the man who approached you in the lobby this afternoon, Baroness?"

"Of course not. I'd never seen him before."

"Do you remember a man named Bruno Wald?"

"But of course," she said. "A charming young film actor who visited us about ten years ago. He was drowned, tragically, in a boating accident."

"The man in the lobby didn't remind you of Bruno Wald?"

"No. Why should he?" Charmian asked.

"The man in the lobby, madame, was Bruno Wald's twin brother," Helwig said, quietly.

Charmian's head swiveled his way again. "Twin?"

Helwig's black glasses were directed at Chambrun. "Madame has never been told of Bruno Wald's return to life, or of the shocking story he told his brother, Stephen Wood. It was, of course, entirely false. It would have been distressing to Madame had she heard it."

Charmian's lips parted. "What story? You all seem to know it but me."

"I'll tell you sometime," Sam Culver said, speaking for the first time, "if Herr Helwig permits." He'd caught the curious relationship, too.

Helwig ignored him. "You ask these questions, Mr. Chambrun, because you think this may have been an act of psychotic revenge on the part of Stephen Wood—murdering Puzzi?"

"I thought of it," Chambrun said.

"Do we know where this Stephen Wood lives?" Masters asked, casually.

"You will leave this to Mr. Chambrun, John," Helwig said, and there was steel in his voice.

Charmian was back at us, still standing very erect. "What have you done with Puzzi's remains, Mr. Chambrun?"

"I have them."

"I would like to give him a decent burial," Charmian said. "And now, if you will excuse me—" She turned and literally ran out of the room.

Helwig watched her go. "She was very fond of the little dog," he said.

"And from what I hear, of Bruno Wald," Sam Culver said.

Black glasses turned on him. "What you have heard, Mr. Culver, is a complete fairy story," Helwig said. He smiled, thin and cruel. "Perhaps Mr. Chambrun would be interested in an account of your own relationship with Madame some years ago. He might find the possibility of a revenge motif in that background, too, don't you think?"

I had never seen Sam Culver without his lazy smile near the surface before. His face had gone dead-white. . . .

"She is beyond belief," Chambrun said. He was walking restlessly up and down the thick Oriental rug in his office. Sam Culver was at the sideboard, pouring himself a very stiff slug of bourbon on the rocks. I stood near the office door with Ruysdale, wanting to get back to Shelda and Red Shoes. I hadn't been dismissed.

I glanced at the chair against the wall. Puzzi's remains had been removed.

"Here is a woman," Chambrun said, talking more to himself than to us, "with an incredible history of self-indulgence, debauchery, and cold-blooded villainy. She hasn't a line in her face to show for it. She has on a mask of almost childlike innocence. She looks twenty years old, untouched by life."

"Conscienceless," Sam said, the neck of the bourbon decanter chattering against the rim of his glass.

"The picture of Dorian Grey," Miss Ruysdale said, surprisingly.

"Helwig runs the show," Chambrun said.

Sam took a long swallow of his drink. "Her legal adviser," he said. "I understand he was a brilliant criminal lawyer in prewar Germany."

Chambrun turned on him. "Do I have to beg you, or do you tell me?'"

"Tell you?"

"What the bloody hell Helwig was talking about—finding a revenge motif in your past relationship with Charmian Zetterstrom."

"Charmian Brown," Sam said, staring at the brown liquor in his glass. "That was her name when I knew her. Zetterstrom hadn't been heard of in those days."

"So, I beg!" Chambrun said, angrily.

Sam looked at him, and his gentle eyes were haggard. He looked, suddenly, very tired.

"Do you believe for an instant, Pierre, that I slaughtered that little dog?"

"Don't be absurd."

"Well, that's something, at any rate," Sam said. He hesitated, and then went back to the sideboard and filled his glass to the brim again. He came over and dropped down wearily into the high-backed armchair by Chambrun's desk. The tired eyes turned toward Ruysdale and me as though he wished we weren't there.

"I'll be in the outer office if you need me, Mr. Chambrun," Ruysdale said.

"No, don't go, Miss Ruysdale." Sam's smile was wry. "I know whatever I tell Pierre in confidence will be repeated to you and Mark. He has no secrets from you two if the subject relates even remotely to the Beaumont."

"And does it?" Chambrun asked.

"In the sense that Charmian and I are both guests of the hotel."

Somehow I wanted to get out of there more than ever before. I didn't want to hear confessions from Sam. But I had no choice. Ruysdale and I exchanged uncomfortable glances. I could see she felt the same way. Chambrun didn't acknowledge our presence by so much as an eye-blink. He didn't offer to send us away, which would have been a courtesy to a friend like Sam. He walked around and sat down behind his desk, his eyes hidden behind the heavy lids. Ruysdale walked over to the sideboard and brought him a demitasse of his Turkish coffee. Then she went to the far end of the paneled room and sat down somewhere in the shadows. Reluctantly I appropriated the chair where Puzzi's mangled body had recently rested.

"My father was an ordained Episcopal minister," Sam said. "Joshua Culver." The old, lazy smile suddenly reappeared. "The Culver men were all named after Old Testament prophets. My grandfather was Micah; my father, Joshua; I am Samuel; my brother, who was killed in Korea, was Jeremiah. They were not as burdensome as some nonsensical namings. They all contracted nicely— Mike, Josh, Sam, Jerry. But they do suggest the kind of strict moral background of the Culvers.

"My father gave up the active ministry fairly early in his career to go into teaching at a famous boys' school in northwest Connecticut, and by the time I was old enough to know what time of day it was he'd become the headmaster. He became a kind of legend in his time, a stern man, but with wit, and enormous sympathy for and understanding of the adolescent male. He was a great man, my father. I thought so then and I think so now.

"One of the most important trustees of the school was a man named Huntingdon Brown. He lived in the school town, gave a large financial gift to the school annually, and made no bones of the fact that he had left several million dollars to the school in his will. He was a widower with one daughter—Charmian. He was strait-laced as an old-fashioned corset. Quite often he was invited to conduct the services in the school chapel. Charmian was the apple of his eye and, in his rose-colored perspective, an angel.

"Even as a little girl she was beautiful—but not an angel. We were the same age, but she was ready to explore the mysteries of sex long before I was. At age eleven she persuaded me to play 'doctor' with her under her father's front porch." Sam chuckled. "At least I discovered the differences between the male and female bodies. She was always climbing around in older men's laps, including my father's. My father was like an uncle to her. Actually, she was brought up to call him Uncle Josh. There were many occasions when old man Brown had to go away on business trips. There was a housekeeper to look after Charmian, but it was dull for her and my mother often suggested that Charmian stay with us when her father was

60

away. I think my mother and father thought of her as sort of an extra child.

"She was mischievous and full of fun, but she could be cruel. She wouldn't hesitate to make us kids look bad in a situation if it would help draw attention to herself. She was a fantastic show-off. At age ten she announced that she was going to be the world's greatest actress, and so far as I know she never changed her mind until Conrad Zetterstrom came along. But I'm getting ahead of myself.

"One summer, when Charmian was sixteen, she came to stay with us during an absence of her father's. She was something pretty exciting by then—a woman, squirming with eagerness to be fulfilled. At sixteen I was a gawky, fumbling nothing, and my brother Jerry, three years younger, didn't figure in things at all. I've never forgotten that first night of Charmian's proposed visit. I think you'll see why.

"It was a sultry August evening, steaming-hot, with a rumbling threat of thunderstorms in the air. Charmian and I played Ping-pong on the screen-porch, of all things. Half a dozen times as we scrambled after an elusive ball she managed to make bodily contact with me, rubbing her very female figure against my skin and bones. I was too stupid to react with anything but embarrassment.

"Eventually we all went to bed. I remember waking up in the middle of the night and realizing that the long threatened thunderstorm had hit us. The rain was pouring down, and the wind was whipping at the window curtains. I saw that it was raining in my window and I got up and paddled across a wet floor to close the window. I was just heading back for bed when I heard a wild screaming coming from somewhere down the hall. It sounded as though someone were being murdered in cold blood.

"I grabbed my bathrobe and ran out into the hall, where the screaming was ear-piercing. I saw my father, in pajamas and bathrobe, coming out of the room where Charmian was supposed to be sleeping. And the screams came from there. It was Charmian who was screaming.

"My mother, also in dressing gown, came out of her and father's room.

" 'What is it, Josh?' she asked.

" 'Damned little idiot,' my father said.

"My mother didn't wait for anything more. She ran down the hall to Charmian's room and went in, closing the door. The screaming stopped and was replaced by the sounds of hysterical weeping and my mother's low, urgent voice.

"My father looked dazed. He became aware of me and came slowly toward me.

" 'What scared her, father?' I asked him.

"He shook his head from side to side. 'It was raining in on that side of the house,' he said. 'I went in to close her windows. She was frightened of the storm. I sat down on the edge of her bed to comfort her, as I have done all through her childhood.' His laugh was harsh. 'Only a little while ago she used to ask for a story to go to sleep by. When she was reassured I bent down to kiss her good night, as I have a thousand times before, she grabbed hold of me and started to scream.'

" 'Still frightened by the storm,' I said.

"My father gave me a bewildered look. His voice was harsh. 'The miserable little bitch says I tried to molest her,' he said. 'That's what she's telling your mother now.'

"It just didn't make sense to me. I knew my father wasn't capable of any such monstrous thing. We stood there in the hall, he looking as though someone had slugged him. Then my mother came out of Charmian's room. She was paper-white. She came straight up to my father.

" 'She's calling her father in New York,' my mother said. 'I couldn't dissuade her.'

"My father's voice shook. 'Elizabeth, you know—'

" 'Of course I know,' my mother said. I remember she touched his face with her fingers."

Sam drew a deep breath. "It's a long story and I needn't bother you with much more of the detail," he said. "Huntingdon Brown came back that night—or early morning. He listened to Charmian's story and she convinced him. Charmian, he said, was incapable of lying about such a thing. Nothing my father or mother would say would convince him otherwise. I knew, and my mother and father both knew, that the only thing she was incapable of was the truth—about this or anything else. She was—is—a congenital liar.

"Late the next afternoon at an emergency meeting of the school's trustees, my father was forced to resign his post as headmaster. There was no publicity in the press, but the story spread like a grass fire. The whole community assumed that my father was a lecherous old goat, guilty of criminal assault against a minor. Criminal charges weren't brought because Huntingdon Brown wanted to protect his daughter from public disgrace.

"The house we lived in belonged to the school, and in the space of a few days we had to move a collection of possessions accumulated over the years. But move to where? It became instantly apparent that my father was to be hounded by Brown; that he could never find himself a job in any school or college, and certainly couldn't go back to the Church. We had lived all these years on a school teacher's salary plus the various benefits, like the house, provided by the school. There were now no savings, no house, and no salary of any sort in prospect.

"An old friend of my father's who believed him offered him a house, rent-free, in California. We disposed of most of our belongings and took the trip west. The house was near Hollywood. I got a job in one of the studios. My mother did baby-sitting and housekeeping chores for one of the lesser film actresses. There was nothing for my father. Somehow the word had followed us to California. He couldn't even get a job cutting grass. They were afraid he might molest one of their children, for Godsake! Poor, dear man.

"One day I came home from work. On the dining-room table there was a note from my mother, saying she was spending the night with the actress' children and telling what there was for supper for my father and Jeremiah and me. No one else was at home, it seemed. I went up to my room and found a note propped up on my bureau, written in my father's strong, distinctive hand. It instructed me not to let my mother go down into the cellar. It said he loved me, and that he was sorry, but there was simply no way out for him.

"I raced down into the cellar and found him hanging by his belt from a furnace pipe. He'd been dead for quite some time."

Sam looked at us. I think we were all stone statues. He got up and went over to the sideboard to refill his glass. No one spoke. Finally he came back and sat down again.

"This is not the time to discuss the morality of suicide," he said, "but my father was driven to it by that bitch. But do you know, as time went on, I began to be gnawed by doubts. If he was innocent, why? He had the bulwark of his religion. He had the belief and faith in him of his family. It was a hard time, but where had his courage gone? I knew Charmian. I knew she would do it in Macy's window to attract attention to herself. I began to wonder if perhaps my father hadn't made love to her. Oh, she'd have relished it from anyone. Then she'd decided to make her own special, murderous capital out of it. It began to grow more certain in my mind that only a secret guilt could have driven my father to kill himself. He had been a hero figure, a God figure, to me. The doubts about him were like a painful growth in my gut.

"Well, time went on. About four years after my father's death things had begun to break for me at the studio. I'd got into publicity, and then, when I'd just passed my twenty-first birthday, I sold a story to one of the big independent producers. From then on I was economically secure. I was wined and dined by the Hollywood elite as one of the 'bright young men.' It was while I was riding that first crest of success that I read in *Variety*, the show-business bible, that a young actress named Charmian Brown, who'd created a small stir in some off-Broadway production, had been signed to a contract by one of the major studios. She'd always said she'd be the greatest, and evidently she was on her way."

Sam took time out to make himself his third drink. His eyes were very bright, but the color had completely drained from his face.

"The doubts about my father were suddenly very much alive again, very painful," Sam said, when he'd resettled in his chair. "I told myself that when Charmian got to Hollywood I'd see her and settle my doubts.

"She was elusive for a while. She'd arrived with considerable fanfare for a nobody, and I heard that she was very rich. Huntingdon Brown had died and left her a very substantial part of his huge fortune. From the very beginning she's always been able to buy what she wanted, even before Conrad Zetterstrom." Sam shifted in his chair. "That isn't quite accurate, because she was never able to buy herself a career as an actress. The trouble was, she just wasn't very good. But in those first few months that she was in Hollywood that hadn't yet been revealed. She was beautiful, photogenic, she'd had one set of good notices off-Broadway, and she'd sleep in any bed that might do her career some good.

"When we first met at a party somewhere she brushed me off in a hurry. I was, she figured, a nobody, a kid she'd grown up with. But after a while she got the message somewhere. I was an important young writer.

"She called me on the phone one day, and invited me to her apartment for dinner. God, she was so transparent. She'd learned that I might be some use to her. The dinner was an intimate tête à tête by candlelight. She talked gaily about our childhood, the old days, never once coming anywhere near the basic tragedy that lay between us. I bided my time. I thought I knew what was going to happen, and I thought I knew when the right time would come to ask the question I had to ask.

"A little while after dinner she came directly to the point.

"'I know you've always wanted to make love to me, Sam,' she said. 'If you'd still like me to, I'd like to—very much.'

"Direct and to the point, our Charmian. We made love. It was a stunning piece of pure sexual techniques." Sam drew a deep breath. "All the time I was waiting for the time when we'd lie side by side, mutually exhausted. When it came—that relaxed moment—I asked her, enormously casual.

"'Did my father really make a pass at you that night, Charmian?'

"She snuggled close to me. 'I'm sorry about Uncle Josh, Sam. I never dreamed——'

" 'Never dreamed what?'

" 'That he'd go to such lengths.'

" 'As to kill himself?'

"She nodded.

" 'But did he do what you accused him of doing?'

"She laughed. 'Of course not. I suppose it was naughty of me, Sam, but you know how I am. Anything to be on camera.' "

Sam's voice shook. "I—I got up out of that monstrous bed. I remember looking down at her, wondering if I ought to kill her as she lay there, naked, smiling up at me. Then I dressed and ran. I was so close to murder I couldn't trust myself."

Sam put down his glass and began to fumble in his pocket for a pipe and pouch.

"I'm not proud of the rest of it," he said. "You have to understand how much I loved my father to understand the fierce hatred I felt for this gal who'd done him in, made me doubt him.

"I went to work on Charmian. I spread the story here and there, judiciously. Some of the important powerhouses who'd romped around in that mammoth bed were suddenly on the run. She was dangerous. I was responsible for their knowing it. She wasn't a good actress, so no one was willing to risk giving her a chance just for the kicks involved in knowing her sexually. Charmian Brown's career died a-borning, and I was responsible. A German director who was doing something in Hollywood decided to run the Charmian risk, but only on his home ground. He signed her for a small part in a movie to be made in Germany. Unless I'm very much mistaken, that film starred Bruno Wald. That may have been when she was first attracted to him.

"I don't know exactly what happened after that. Either the German director gave her the bounce, or she him. Anyhow, somewhere in that segment of time she met old Conrad Zetterstrom. The next I heard of her was that she'd married the Baron and gone to live on his island. I never saw her again until this afternoon."

Sam looked up over the flame of the lighter he was holding to his pipe. "That, Pierre, is the story Helwig was referring to. As for its supplying me with a revenge motif—I can only tell you it doesn't. It's all past and done with. My father's image was restored and remains intact in my memory. If I feel anything at all, it's a small sense of guilt for what I did to her back there in Hollywood. But, by God, she had it coming to her."

There was a long silence, and then Chambrun asked: "Did she mention it to you today—now—when you went to see her?"

"Oh, she mentioned it," Sam said. His laugh was short and bitter. "Trust Charmian! But there's no way to bring my father up out of that cellar." He shook himself, like a dog coming out of water. "I'm going out for a walk," he said. "I need to get some fresh air into my lungs." . . .

I went looking for Shelda and found a note from her on my desk. It said, in effect, that she'd gotten tired of waiting for me, and if I cared to know what her relationship was, and promised to be, with young Mr. Peter Wynn, I might drop by her place some time. The bitch!

I was just about to lock up my office and head for my apartment to change for the evening when Mr. Amato, the Beaumont's banquet manager, poked his head in my office door.

"Got a minute, Mr. Haskell?" he asked.

Mr. Amato is a tall, dark, thin man in his early forties. He is a Roman, and he must have been a very beautiful young man with a profile like a god on a coin. There were now little puffs and pouches and lines that suggested dyspepsia and incipient ulcers. I knew that the top of his desk in his own private office was a small apothecary shop, loaded with all kinds of soothing medicines, the kind that coat and the kind that don't coat, the kind that effervesce and the kind that go down like a milky chalk. I knew that three quarters of his daily intake was medicinal, not caloric.

"I wanted to talk to you for a moment about the Baroness Zetterstrom," Amato said.

"Who doesn't?" I said. I was, frankly, up to there with the lady. The two stories we'd heard about her from Sam Culver had left me with a strong feeling of revulsion for Charmian Zetterstrom. Her unnaturally preserved youth added an unhealthy dividend to a potion of sadistic villainy. I had the feeling that to be in her presence was to risk contamination, and I quietly hated myself because of a strong impulse to go to see her again. I would have denied that under oath to Shelda, but there it was. Evil has, unfortunately, a diabolical fascination for most of us that the Ten Commandments lack.

"I want to know what she is like," Amato said.

"Oh, brother!"

"I mean, does she really know food and wines? Is she a genuine connoisseur, or is she simply a rich show-off?"

"I think she might even be able to tell you whether human flesh tastes better broiled or roasted," I said.

"My God!" Amato said.

"Seriously, I suspect you can't fake this dinner, Amato. Her palate is almost certainly educated."

Amato giggled. "I remember advice from Mr. Chambrun on another occasion," he said. "Kangaroo tail soup, specially flown in from Australia. It is unbelievably foul-tasting, but the guests will eat every last drop of it, smacking their lips, lest somebody should guess that they have no experience of exotic dishes."

"I think if it wasn't delicious the lady would complain," I said. "I don't think her aim is to impress."

Amato took a slip of paper out of his pocket. "Aged beef is a problem these days," he said. "I was prepared to suggest roast venison *grand veneur*. I would precede it with special salmon flown in from the Canadian Northwest."

"I think you should discuss it with the Baroness," I said. "It will keep you from guessing. I think she is altogether capable of saying yes or no. It should save you a lot of anxiety—and at least three Bromo Seltzers."

"You think I will not find her difficult?" he asked, little beads of sweat showing on his long upper lip.

"I think you will find her unlike anyone you've dealt with before, chum. But I suggest you put off seeing her at least until tomorrow. She's in an unhappy state this evening."

"The dog. I heard about the dog," Amato said. "It's unbelievable."

"I saw it," I said.

"Thank God it was not me," Amato said, his ulcer obviously twitching. "Thank you for your advice, Mr. Haskell."

"I hope I haven't misled you," I said.

At the door Amato turned back. "With the kangaroo tail soup you serve a Madeira sercial," he said.

For a man who couldn't eat food his obsession with it was slightly comic. . . .

Shelda has moments of infantilism. They appear almost always when she's mad at me and thinks she can get even by making me jealous. She was reading a copy of *Life* when I let myself into her apartment. Have I admitted that I have a key?

"He's really quite masculine," she said, not looking up.

"Who? Cary Grant?"

"Don't be a dope!" she said. "I'm talking about Peter Wynn, of course."

"You have reason to be certain?"

She gave me an evil little grin. "I was offered the opportunity."

"Fast worker, your Mr. Wynn."

"At the crucial moment we were interrupted," Shelda said. And then she stopped playing games. "Oh, Mark, who could have done such a thing to that poor little dog?"

"Someone not nice," I said. "Was the news of that what interrupted Mr. Wynn's pass at you?"

"Don't be a jerk," Shelda said. "He didn't make a pass at me. He was politely admiring, which does a girl good."

"How did he take the news about Puzzi?"

"He said, 'That sonofabitch!' and left me flat."

"Which sonofabitch?"

"He didn't say. Do they know who did it, Mark?"

"Not yet," I said. "But depend on Chambrun and Jerry. They'll find out." I lit a cigarette. "There are no lines or wrinkles," I said. "Can you suggest how she does it?"

"Monkey glands," she said, bitterly.

"They went out in the twenties."

"She's hooked you!"

"Yes and no," I said. "She's fascinating. She's also scary." I made us a pair of Scotch on the rocks, and then I brought her up to date. It took two drinks to get through Sam's stories about Charmian, with Shelda interrupting like the commercials on TV. I'd just finished the story of Sam's father when the telephone rang. Shelda answered and then handed the phone to me. "Jerry Dodd for you."

"You've found the dognapper?" I asked him.

"We've graduated to people," he said, in a strange, hard

voice. I scarcely recognized it.

"What do you mean?"

"The Baroness' maid," he said. "The little blond dish they call Heidi."

"What about her?"

"She went to the corner drugstore to do an errand for the Baroness. Someone grabbed her, dragged her into an alley, bashed in her skull, and slashed her to pieces with a dull knife."

"Like Puzzi!" I said. My mouth was cotton-dry.

"Like Puzzi," Jerry said. "You better get over here."

Part Two

1

As I've said before, a big hotel like the Beaumont is in reality a small town in itself. The same things happen in it that happen in any other town; births, natural deaths, suicides, fires, divorces, clandestine love affairs, robberies, business failures, celebrations, funerals—and murder.

Technically, the murder of the girl named Heidi had probably not taken place in the hotel. I say probably not because her body had been found a block away in an alley, and so far there was no indication that it had been carried there from somewhere else, like the hotel. But the dramatis personae were very much a part of the hotel. The police investigation would be centered there with Charmian Zetterstrom and her curious staff. The story would make a field day for the news media, and the Beaumont would come in for an unwanted chunk of lurid publicity. My job, I knew, as I hurried back to the hotel from Shelda's, would be to soft-pedal that aspect of it as best I could.

The lobby looked normally quiet for eight o'clock in the evening, but I'd noticed two police cars parked down the block from the entrance as I came in.

Karl Nevers, the night reservation man, was on duty at the desk and I hurried over to him.

"The boss's office," he said, before I got out a question. "Hardy's with him."

As I headed for the elevators, Mike Maggio, the night bell captain, flagged me down. Mike has a gamin Italian face that's usually screwed up in a mischievous grin. He looked very serious at this moment.

"I'm looking for the long-haired one," Mike said. "You seen him?"

"What long-haired one?"

"The one with the red pants. Wynn, his name is. He's missing. Hardy wants him."

"I haven't seen him since six o'clock when he was buying a drink for Shelda in the Trapeze."

Mike's mischievous grin wrinkled his face. "Shelda's in good form, I hope," he said.

"Keep your nose out of my business," I said, grinning back at him.

I took the elevator to the second floor and headed for Chambrun's office. "Hardy" was Lieutenant Hardy, a big, dark young man with an athletic build who looks more like a good-natured, if slightly puzzled, college fullback than a Homicide detective. We could be grateful for small mercies. We'd had Hardy with us before. He knew Chambrun and the inner workings of the hotel. He would know who to trust in our setup and wouldn't waste a lot of time suspecting people like Mrs. Kniffen, the housekeeper, or some other innocent on the staff.

Hardy was with Chambrun and Miss Ruysdale in the inner office. He gave me a friendly nod as I came in. I saw that Chambrun had a set of file cards on his desk. They must be the ones relating to Charmian and her crew.

"Sorry to inconvenience you," Chambrun said, drily. "The Lieutenant is anxious to find out what he can about the Zetterstrom mob before he starts on a questioning bee. We don't have much on file except rumors."

"We have Sam Culver," I said.

"Sam has gone out somewhere for the evening. No reason he should have told us where he was going."

"I understand Peter Wynn is among the missing."

"I half hoped we might find him with you and Shelda," Chambrun said.

They say at the Beaumont that Chambrun must have some secret peepholes that allow him to see everything that's going on everywhere at the same time. He was obviously aware that Peter Wynn had been in the Trapeze with Shelda and me.

"You've got some kind of a nut prowling the joint," Hardy said, scowling. "Only a sick mind could do the kind of job that was done on the girl—and the dog!"

"Murder always involves a sick mind," Chambrun said.

"What actually happened to the girl?" I said. "No one's told me."

"Another dog story," Hardy said. "Woman walking a

Pekingese. It started to bark and raise hell at the mouth of an alley down the street. The woman investigated and found the girl. Horror stuff. She was ripped to pieces, head smashed in. Lady had presence of mind enough to call the cops instead of running off screaming by herself. Quick identification. The girl hadn't been robbed. Eighty-ninety dollars in her handbag, and the key to her room in the Beaumont. We knew who she was in ten minutes. Heidi Brunner."

"She's the Amazon's daughter," Chambrun said.

"She went out to get a prescription for sleeping pills filled—for the Baroness," Hardy said. "Never got to the drugstore. The prescription was still in her handbag, signed by Dr. Malinkov."

"He's licensed to practice here?" I asked.

Hardy nodded. "He was a top-flight plastic surgeon during World War II. Brought here from Germany toward the end of the war to work on mutilated G.I.'s. Licensed then. He went back to Europe in 1950. Evidently became part of the Zetterstrom world about that time."

Chambrun glanced at me. "May explain the lady's lack of wrinkles," he said.

The red button on Chambrun's desk phone began to blink. Ruysdale answered, listened, then covered the mouthpiece with her hand.

"It's Marcus Helwig," she said. "Both the Baroness and Madame Brunner are in hysterics. He knows the police are about to descend on them. He asks for the chance to answer preliminary questions away from them. Can he come here?"

"God save me from hysterical women," Hardy said. "Tell him to come. Let me talk to my man there."

One of Hardy's assistants was already in the Zetterstrom quarters getting routine information. Hardy told him to send along a police stenographer with Helwig. Without waiting for instructions Ruysdale set up a small table and a chair for the stenotype operator at the far side of the room.

"Thing I don't like about this," Hardy said, "is the pattern. When you have a repeated M.O. you learn to expect a sort of chain reaction."

"M.O. meaning modus operandi," Chambrun said.

"Meaning method of operation," Hardy said. "Dog and woman—same pattern. Like you ask yourself, who's next?"

Helwig arrived with the police stenographer while Ruysdale was preparing a fresh demitasse for Chambrun. Helwig's eyes were hidden by the black glasses. The grim lines at the corners of his mouth were etched deep, as though a sculptor had chiseled them in stone.

"I appreciate your courtesy in seeing me here," he said. "As you can imagine, Madame Brunner is distraught. The girl was her daughter. The Baroness was very fond of the girl. She's had her as a personal maid for some years. She is shocked, and a little frightened, I think."

"Frightened?" Chambrun asked, his heavy eyelids lifting.

"Is it unreasonable for her to imagine that this is some sort of attack on *her?*" Helwig asked. "First her precious dog, then her close personal maid."

"This afternoon in the lobby, when there was the commotion with Stephen Wood, the Baroness said, 'I have been in some danger recently.' What did she mean? Why, to come to the point, does she have a bodyguard?"

Helwig took a silver cigarette case from his breast pocket. I saw that it was an exact duplicate of the one carried by Peter Wynn. Merry Christmas from the Zetterstroms? "It is permitted to smoke?" he asked, and took a cigarette from the case and lit it with a silver lighter when Hardy nodded. "Surely, Mr. Chambrun, you are aware of some of the circumstances surrounding extraordinary wealth. The Baroness has one of the largest private fortunes in the world today. She's automatically a target for confidence men, thieves, the operators of dishonest charities, but most of all, for revolutionary crackpots who simply feel she should be eliminated because she is rich. If she had children they'd have to be guarded day and night from people who would see them as prime objects for a kidnapping venture."

"There are other reasons," Chambrun said, in a cold voice.

Helwig nodded, as if to acknowledge a reasonableness in Chambrun's statement. "Baron Zetterstrom was a much-hated man," he said. "I don't choose to rise to his defense at this moment. But I concede that every Jew who remembers, or has been taught to remember, Hitler-Germany hated him with a passion. Hated him and everything that was his—including his wife. He was unconventional in the way he lived after the war. There are moralists and religious fanatics who hated him, hate his memory, and hate what is left of his world—including his wife. There are people who attempted to ingratiate themselves with the Baron and Baroness on the Island, dreaming of financial gain, who found themselves tossed out into the night. They hate the Baron's memory—and his wife."

"And there are the Bruno Walds of those days," Chambrun said.

Helwig's stone mask didn't alter by a hair. "Yes, there are the Bruno Walds," he said. "They too hate the Baroness. Does that answer your question as to why a bodyguard, Mr. Chambrun?" He inhaled a deep lungful of smoke and looked around, tentatively, for an ashtray. Ruysdale was at his elbow with one. "When irrational violence appears on stage with the Baroness she has reason to fear that she may be the eventual target. *I* fear it. I shall urge her to return to the Island, where we can guarantee her safety."

"Since the lady has so many enemies," Hardy said, "and since you have evidently been close to the situation for a long time——"

"I was the Baron's legal adviser before the war," Helwig said. "Thirty years—and, of course, all the twenty years of his marriage and until today. I serve the Baroness as I served the Baron."

"Then you must be closely aware of who her enemies

may be," Hardy said.

The corner of Helwig's mouth twitched. "Do you ask me to pick a murderer for you out of all the population of Israel? Do you ask me to pick one out of a half-million prisoners of war from all the nations of the world who suffered under his wartime disciplines? Do you ask me to pick a murderer out of scores of people who were damaged by the Baron and Baroness' way of life and from their hundreds of scores of sympathetic relatives and friends? All I can do, Lieutenant, is listen for the stealthy footstep outside her door, for a face across a crowded room that inadvertently reveals the fires of hatred. I know only that there is danger all around her and that it was sheer idiocy for her to leave the Island. But she insisted."

"And you haven't heard that stealthy footstep or seen that face here?" Hardy asked. There was irony in his question. He hated what he called "fancy talk."

Helwig hesitated. "There was Stephen Wood in the lobby this afternoon," he said. "There is Samuel Culver, who hates her."

I thought I heard a faint grunt of impatience from Chambrun. I glanced at him. His eyes seemed to be closed.

"They can, of course, be checked out," Hardy said.

"I trust you will be able to."

"I understand Mr. Culver was with the Baroness when the dog was found."

"When the dog was found," Helwig said. "But may he not have encountered Puzzi on his way to visit the Baroness, killed him, crammed him into a trash can, and then calmly rung the Baroness' doorbell?"

"Oh, for Godsake," Chambrun said, impatiently.

"And why would he kill the maid?" Hardy asked.

"To strike cold terror to the Baroness' heart."

"He'd commit a brutal murder just to make the Baroness nervous?"

"The art of torture," Helwig said, "is based on the theory of stretching out for as long as possible the period of pain and fear."

"You should know," Chambrun said, suddenly angry. "You were Conrad Zetterstrom's chief aide, and he was the master."

"Yes, Mr. Chambrun, I should know," Helwig said, unruffled.

"You pick on Wood and Culver simply because they are the only people here you know have reason to hate the Baroness?" Hardy asked.

"Yes."

"But there could be someone else?"

"There could be many others I wouldn't recognize by sight," Helwig said. "You see how real the danger is? If I can persuade the Baroness, do I have your permission to take her immediately back to the Island?"

"When we have Heidi Brunner's killer safely locked away. That's when you can go places, Mr. Helwig."

There was a moment of silence. Then Chambrun glanced at Hardy. "May I?" he asked.

"Fire away," Hardy said.

Chambrun's bright, bold eyes looked at Helwig from

under their heavy lids. "Did Heidi Brunner have any reason to kill the dog?" he asked.

"Why on earth——?" Helwig sounded genuinely startled.

Chambrun shrugged. "She was the dog's nursemaid," he said. "She might not have shown it openly, but she could have detested the little beast."

"But—she didn't kill herself," Helwig said. "And I think she was genuinely fond of Puzzi. He was a nice little dog."

"I am remembering a scene at which you were present, Herr Helwig," Chambrun said. "When I had reported the death of the dog to the Baroness, she said, 'An eye for an eye! Whoever did it will be made to suffer just as Puzzi suffered.'"

"But that was an extravagant—"

"I got the impression that Masters was quite ready to follow those instructions to the letter."

"My dear sir—"

"Don't look so wide-eyed and innocent, Herr Helwig. The suggestion was made. It could very well have been followed out. The dog's skull was crushed, his body slashed by a dull knife. The girl's skull was crushed, her body slashed by a dull knife."

"What about this Masters guy?" Hardy asked.

"He's a psychotic," Chambrun said. "You don't need a degree in psychiatry to spot it. He goes into action without giving it a moment's thought. He could have killed Stephen Wood in the lobby this afternoon with that karate blow to the throat. He'd have made an old-time Western gunslinger blush with shame at the speed he had a gun into action. I was looking straight into his eyes when he pulled that gun, and I tell you my life was in the balance for about two seconds."

"What about that gun?" Hardy asked. "It's a violation of the Sullivan law."

"He's licensed to carry it," Helwig said. He sounded suddenly very tired. The lines at the corners of his grim mouth seemed to be chiseled deeper into his gray face.

"How could he be?" Hardy asked. "You just got in at Kennedy this afternoon. He hasn't left the Baroness to go get himself licensed."

"It was arranged for in advance," Helwig said. "The authorities recognized that the Baroness was in need of a bodyguard."

"Goddamned gun laws," Hardy muttered.

"You're evading my question, Herr Helwig," Chambrun said. "Is it possible that Heidi Brunner killed the dog and that Masters punished her for it? An eye for an eye, despite my insistence that we be allowed to handle things?"

"The Baroness instructed him to the contrary," Helwig said. "You heard her."

"The Baroness is a woman. She could have changed her mind."

"I would swear to the contrary," Helwig said.

"What kind of passport did Masters come into the country on?" Hardy asked.

"He's an American citizen," Helwig said.

"Three cheers for the red, white, and blue," Hardy said. "I think I'd like to talk to that guy in a hurry." He headed for the phone on Chambrun's desk.

"Please," Helwig said, "don't have him brought up here until I have returned to the Baroness' suite. I don't want her left unprotected."

"You don't trust the police?" Hardy asked.

"I've learned to trust no one in this world but myself, Lieutenant," Helwig said.

"But you left the Baroness to come here without protesting."

"I trust Masters," Helwig said. "I trust him because I know how to destroy him, and he knows I know how," Helwig said. "No one else."

"Go back to the suite and send him down here," Hardy said.

"Wait!" Chambrun said. "You might save us a lot of evasive answers, Herr Helwig, if you told us just how Masters happened to become a part of the Zetterstrom household."

Helwig hesitated, fumbling for his silver cigarette case. "He was an American prisoner of war back in 1943 or '44," he said. "General Zetterstrom—the Baron was a general, you know—was in charge of the prison camp where Masters was held. Masters—well, he traded favors for favors."

"A stooly?" Hardy asked. "He squealed on the other prisoners, right?"

"He was a kind of voyeur," Helwig said.

"What the hell is that?" Hardy asked.

"I imagine he enjoyed watching people being tortured," Chambrun said. "I know the breed. How often did he bring false charges against a fellow prisoner just for the pleasure of watching him punished?"

Helwig's stony mask of a face didn't alter. "Often, I imagine."

"The Baron must have been fond of him," Chambrun said. "Birds of a feather—."

Helwig shrugged. "The Baron offered Masters a job after the war. Masters accepted and came to the Island."

"Where they could torture people without interference," Chambrun said. "People like Bruno Wald."

Helwig's mouth tightened, but he didn't speak.

"So Masters has been a part of the Zetterstrom picture for more than twenty years?"

"Yes."

"Did he never leave the Island in all that time?"

"Oh, he left frequently. When the Baron wanted business transacted for him in Europe."

"Murder business? There must have been a lot of people who had to be kept quiet."

Again no answer.

"Is it possible Masters was in New York the day Bruno Wald died?" Chambrun asked.

"The day he committed suicide?"

"The day he died," Chambrun said.

"I would have to check my records," Helwig said. "I

don't recall that he was away from the Island at that time."

"But he may have been?"

"I'd have to check my records."

"Is that what you have on Masters, Herr Helwig? The proof that he cut Bruno Wald's throat?"

"You are a very expert inventor of fairy tales, Mr. Chambrun."

"I just wondered," Chambrun said, and turned away to stare moodily into his demitasse.

"Send Masters here," Hardy said.

Helwig gave the room a polite, heel-clicking little bow and was gone.

"God!" Hardy said. "What kind of people are we dealing with?"

"People out of a nightmare," Chambrun said.

The nightmare expanded at that moment. The red button on Chambrun's desk blinked, and Ruysdale, unruffled as always, answered.

"Peter Wynn has just walked into the lobby," she reported to us. "Jerry wants to know if he is to be allowed to go up to the Zetterstrom suite, or if you want him."

"I want him," Hardy said. He turned to Chambrun as Ruysdale instructed Jerry. "Brief me on this one, Chambrun."

Chambrun shrugged. "An uncommonly large number of men prefer to have their needs gratified by prostitutes," he said. "That's why it's one of the oldest professions. But the woman who wants sex without romance is something of a rarity. Charmian Zetterstrom is evidently that rare type.

You've heard the Bruno Wald story. I suppose Mr. Peter Wynn is well paid for his stud services. He apparently doesn't find the work irksome."

"Looking at the Baroness, it's hard to believe," Hardy said. "She looks so fresh. Not jaded, if you know what I mean."

"Looking at the Baroness makes it hard to believe many of the things we know to be facts about her," Chambrun said.

I was surprised by the appearance of Peter Wynn when Jerry brought him into the office. It wasn't just his clothes. The Carnaby Street styling had been abandoned. He was wearing an ordinary charcoal-gray business suit with a blue turtle-neck sweater for a shirt. Only his long red hair would have made him look any different from any young man on the street, and in this day of long hairdos, nobody to look at twice. The thing that really surprised me was the fact that his eyes were red-rimmed, and he looked as if he'd recently been crying. His face was screwed up in the expression you've seen on a small child's face when he's fighting tears.

"Mr. Wynn has been out for a walk—for several hours," Jerry said in his dry, professional voice. "He hadn't heard about Miss Brunner's murder till I told him."

"Oh, God, poor Heidi," Wynn said, and tears welled up into his eyes. "You'll have to forgive me. I was terribly, terribly fond of Heidi."

"Doesn't it beat all hell?" Hardy asked the room at large. "Whenever you have a possible suspect in a murder case he never has an alibi. He was 'just out for a walk.'

God, how people walk when there's a crime being committed. No one ever sees them and can support the alibi. I don't suppose anyone saw you, Wynn?"

"This is the first time I've ever been in New York," Wynn said.

"All right, let's have your version."

"Version of what?" Wynn asked. I realized he had the faint hint of a British accent. Not broad. More like ordinary, good standard stage speech.

"Your several hours of walking," Hardy said.

"We just arrived this afternoon, as you know," Wynn said. "We were to have dined in the Grill Room here at the hotel. Then there was the nastiness about Puzzi. Charmian was badly shaken by it. She canceled out on the dinner. So I was free. As I say, I'd never been in New York, so I thought I'd walk around a bit, take in the theatre district and Broadway, with its lights and all. That's what I did. I understand it isn't what it used to be, but it's still pretty extraordinary from a stranger's point of view."

"We're glad you liked it," Hardy said, drily. "What time was your next obligation to the Baroness?"

"Obligation? I don't follow."

"Surely a little thing like a murder wouldn't interfere with the Baroness' sex life," Hardy said.

Wynn's eyes widened. "Are you suggesting—?"

"Oh, come off it, Mr. Wynn. You know what I'm suggesting. Your job. If she was so upset about the dog, didn't she need your comforting touch?"

"I think I rather resent that," Wynn said. "Just what do you think my job is?"

"Gigolo—or should I spell it for you?"

"You damned idiot!" Wynn said. Then he laughed. "Oh, Lord, that is rather funny, you know."

"What's funny?"

"Because there is just a grain of truth in it."

"I should be grateful for that, I suppose," Hardy said.

"I am paid to act as a public escort for Charmian," Wynn said. "But pay attention to the word 'public,' please. She doesn't like to appear at any sort of public gathering, even in her own home, without a male escort. It keeps her from being the odd woman at a dinner party, for example. It protects her from the many men who look at her with dollar signs in their eyes. I suppose people have thought my job went farther than that, but it doesn't—hasn't ever."

"So, when she decided not to eat in the Grill you were at liberty to take a walk?" Hardy said. He sounded as if he hadn't believed a word of Wynn's story so far.

"Yes."

"You say she was shaken up by the 'nastiness' about the dog?"

"Of course. She was terribly fond of the little fellow."

"And this Heidi girl, did she enjoy being a nursemaid to a pooch?"

"What do you mean, nursemaid?"

"She carried him into the hotel when you arrived," Chambrun said. "She was obviously responsible for him."

"But that was just today," Wynn said. "Coming from the airport. Actually, Puzzi had the run of the Island, of the house there, and would have had the run of the rooms here. No one particularly had charge of him. Charmian actually fed him herself. He was very much her dog."

"So the Heidi girl didn't hate the dog enough to kill it?" Hardy asked.

"Good God, no!"

"Mr. Chambrun thought she might, and that the Baroness had ordered her killer-boy to inflict a little rough justice."

"Utter rot," Wynn said, his voice unsteady.

"Then who hated the Heidi girl enough to kill her in cold blood?"

"It's unbelievable," Wynn said. The tears were close again. "I've heard about the uncontrolled violence in this town, but I never believed——"

"It's a hundred to one the same person who killed the dog killed the girl," Hardy said. "Who hated her that much?"

"No one!" Wynn said. "She was a sweet, kindly, almost totally unsophisticated child. She was born on the Island, you know. This was her first trip away from it in all her life."

"So if she had an enemy he must have come from the Island," Hardy said. "What about you, Wynn? Did you hate her for some reason?"

"You bloody fool!" Wynn said, his voice rising. "Heidi was my girl. We were planning to be married here in New

York. It wasn't possible on the Island—no way to make it legal, no priest, no legal machinery. Tomorrow we planned to apply for a license."

"How did the Baroness feel about that? She would be losing her male escort." You could tell Hardy suddenly smelled a motive.

"Charmian was delighted for both of us," Wynn said. "She'd agreed to stand up with Heidi when the time came."

"Was Killer-boy interested in Heidi?" Hardy asked. "Had she given him the brush?"

Wynn's wide eyes stared past Hardy at the blue Picasso on the wall. "Oh, my God!" he whispered. . . .

If I were to say that John Masters reminded me of Sean Connery, the actor, you would immediately get the impression that there was something romantic about him. Physically, the actor and the bodyguard were alike—slim, tall, muscular, dark, with anything but a baby-face. Masters' wide, thin mouth seemed always ready for a smile that didn't quite come. His eyes were a pale blue and unbelievably cold. I can't quite explain it, but I got the impression of a hunter constantly stalking a prey. There was no such thing as physical fear in him, I thought. I could see that he might be attractive to women, and particularly to a woman like Charmian Zetterstrom who, according to all accounts, would enjoy the sadistic techniques of a man like Masters.

His clothes were obviously custom-tailored, and there

was genius involved in the cut of his jacket, which I knew concealed a gun harness.

"Gentlemen," he said. And then he spotted Ruysdale in the far corner of the room; he gave her a slight, mocking bow. "And Mademoiselle," he said.

He might be American, but there was the faint quality of the professional Irishman in his speech; cultivated, not a thug.

"I want to see your gun," Hardy said, without preamble.

Masters' potential smile remained potential. His hand moved quickly inside his jacket. I saw that his fingers were neatly manicured. But he didn't produce his gun. Instead, he came out with a thin, alligator-skin wallet. He flipped it open and showed it to Hardy.

"My permit to bear arms," he said.

"I didn't ask for your permit. I asked for the gun," Hardy said.

Masters' smile was still a shadow in the background. He produced the gun, a black, shiny automatic, spun it around by the trigger guard, and handed it, butt end outward, to the Lieutenant. Hardy took a handkerchief out of his pocket, wrapped it around the butt end, and dropped the gun in his pocket.

"Now, just a minute," Masters said, quietly.

"The butt of a gun would make an excellent tool for smashing in the skulls of dogs and women," Hardy said. "I'd like the police lab to look at it."

"You're joking," Masters said. His hands hung at his

sides and I could see he kept flexing his fingers.

"The Lieutenant rarely jokes in the face of murder," Chambrun said.

Masters turned his pale eyes toward the Florentine desk. It was quite obvious he considered Chambrun more formidable than the Lieutenant. Perhaps he was remembering that Chambrun had faced him down earlier that day in the lobby.

"I like a man who doesn't flinch in the face of danger," Masters said. "Did you know that gun of mine was hair-trigger ready when you walked into it this afternoon?"

"I knew it wouldn't be fired by accident," Chambrun said.

"How right you are." Masters turned back to Hardy.

"Just what is it you want to ask me, Lieutenant? I don't like to be away from the Baroness for too long. Is it possible you believe I might have killed Puzzi and the girl?"

"It crosses my mind," Hardy said.

"Or at least the girl," Chambrun said. " 'An eye for an eye—.' "

"Ah, yes. The Baroness' impulsive reaction to the news that her little dog had been slaughtered."

"So?" Hardy said.

"So I was instructed to forget that outburst. I forgot it."

"Let's go back to that time," Hardy said. "Chambrun brought the news about the dog. What happened after he left?"

Masters shrugged. "We considered the question of who

might have done it."

"Conclusions?"

"There's been a great deal of coming and going," Masters said. "Bellhops with luggage, room service with drinks, the housekeeper to take the linen sheets off the Baroness' bed and replace them with the silk sheets the Baroness had brought with her. Sometime during those comings and goings Puzzi must have slipped out into the hall. None of us was aware that he was missing. There are eleven rooms in the setup on the nineteenth floor. There are so many places he could have been."

"Did it occur to you that Sam Culver might have killed the dog?" Hardy asked.

"Oh, yes. I asked him."

"And he said—?"

"He said no, of course. I thought I'd ask him again sometime when I could be alone with him."

"Arm-twisting?" Chambrun asked, quietly.

I thought the smile would come to the surface, but it didn't. "Something like that."

"Did you think it might have been Stephen Wood?"

"I thought it possible."

"So the Baroness was upset and she sent Heidi Brunner out to get a prescription for sleeping pills filled."

"My dear fellow, you don't know the Baroness," Masters said. "She doesn't need sleeping pills. She doesn't have nerves. She doesn't have a conscience that bothers her. The pills were for Dr. Malinkov. He has all the things the Baroness doesn't have."

"Why didn't he get the pills for himself?"

Masters' pale eyes seemed to get brighter. "He didn't want to go out on the street alone."

"Why not?"

"In the old days of the war the good doctor performed some rather interesting experiments on human guinea pigs," Masters said, as though he remembered it with pleasure. "He's afraid someone who resented it might recognize him. It took a great deal of persuasion to get him to leave the Island. I suspect he needs the pills because he has nightmares about the old days."

"And you don't?"

"No. It was all part of an interesting social experiment."

"I've never heard it called that," Hardy said, anger in his voice.

"At the time it seemed justified in terms of a long-range future that didn't come off."

"But there was no reason to think it was dangerous for the girl to go out on the street alone?"

"There was no reason to suppose it. As it turned out, of course, there was." Masters sounded completely indifferent.

"You didn't follow her out?"

"No."

"Proof?"

"The Baroness, Helwig, Madame Brunner—they all know I didn't leave the suite."

"At any rate, they'll all say so."

"They'll certainly all say so."

"How do you usually react to being turned down by a young lady to whom you offer your unusual physical charms?" Chambrun asked. His eyes were narrowed against a curl of smoke from his Egyptian cigarette.

"The nature of my job doesn't give me much opportunity for sexualizing—if that's the word for what you mean," Masters said.

"But Heidi Brunner did give you the brush-off, didn't she, Masters? What happened? Did she complain to the Baroness about your passes?"

Masters seemed to freeze for a moment. "Peter's been at it, I see."

"He told us nothing, but he reacted to a question," Chambrun said.

I could almost see Masters making a mental note to do something about Peter Wynn. "Heidi was born on the Island," he said. "I was in the next room with the Baron when they spanked her behind and she let out her first squawk. She was a little child, running around underfoot. I never thought of her as anything but a child. Hell, she's—she was—not quite twenty!"

"It has been called the Lolita fetish," Chambrun said.

"You're a cool sonofabitch," Masters said, without anger. He grinned. "I've never run across a man I was afraid of, Chambrun. But Clara Brunner is something else! Throw one off-color glance at her child and you'd face one of the original Furies. It wouldn't have been worth the risk, interesting as Heidi might have been. Clara was one of the Baron's favorites. I'd have lost my job."

"Clara Brunner didn't object to the prospect of Heidi's marrying Peter Wynn?"

"Marriage made everything all right for Clara. She never had it herself." Masters smiled as he saw the question in Chambrun's eyes. "Didn't you know? Heidi was Baron Zetterstrom's illegitimate spawn. Oh, Clara was a handsome woman twenty years ago."

"Let's get back to tonight," Hardy said. "The girl was sent out to the drugstore. She didn't come back. Were none of you concerned?"

"My dear Lieutenant, the local fuzz is so wonderfully efficient that there wasn't time for us to miss Heidi before your boys came charging in with the news that she'd been liquidated."

I don't think I ever heard anyone talk so without emotion about the death of another human being who'd been remotely close. Hardy had had it.

"Well, hysterics or no hysterics, I'm going up to talk to the two women," he said.

Masters actually laughed. "If you anticipate hysterics, Lieutenant, you're in for a disappointment. Hysterics are not in the Baroness' nature, and Clara, the old battle-axe, is hard as a rock."

"Helwig told us they were in no condition to be questioned."

"Then Marcus was stalling for time," Masters said.

"Time for what?"

Masters shrugged. "There's no way to guess what that

most devious of humans is up to at any time," he said.

Hardy's slow burn was reaching the explosion point. "We've pussyfooted around long enough," he said. "Let's get up to the nineteenth floor." He started for the door.

"Just a minute, Lieutenant," Masters said. "My gun. If you're taking it to the police lab, what do I do about a gun? I can't do my job without one. Feel naked, as a matter of fact."

"Then wrap yourself up in something," Hardy said, and was gone.

2

When Chambrun, Hardy, Masters, and I reached the nineteenth floor we were greeted outside the elevator by one of Hardy's men, a Homicide detective by the name of Molloy. He looked at Masters, uncertainly, then took Hardy by the arm and led him a few steps down the hall. Chambrun and Masters and I couldn't hear the conversation at the time, but a few minutes later Chambrun and I knew that Molloy and his men had come on something. The service elevator at the end of the hall had been checked out as a matter of routine, and fresh bloodstains were found on the floor of the car. It was possible they had no connection with the murder, but a sample had been rushed off to the police lab to check the blood type against the dead girl's.

It was possible, Molloy told Hardy, for the body to have been taken down in the service elevator and carried, through a maze of back alleys, to the spot where it had been found without its ever being taken out onto the street. It would explain something that had been bothering the Homicide men—how, at eleven o'clock at night when the area around the Beaumont was still pretty busy, the girl could have been attacked out in the open without anyone seeing or hearing a thing. The risk to the murderer would have been enormous. The cops were not even considering the possibility of some lunatic purse-snatcher. The M.O., as Hardy had described it, were identical in the cases of the dog and the girl—separated by several hours. It suggested someone hanging around with a very specific plan in mind.

Molloy wanted everyone out of the Zetterstrom rooms so his men could fine-tooth-comb the place. No matter how carefully the evidence of a bloody killing had been cleaned up, a scientific search should reveal evidence of it. Hardy bought Molloy's idea. He came back and gave us the story. I saw Masters purse his lips in a sort of silent whistle.

Helwig answered Hardy's bell-ring at the door of 19-B.

"I want everyone out of these rooms for a while," Hardy said.

The gray man's face was marble-hard. "I think that's out of the question," he said. "Why do you want us out?"

"Search," Hardy said. "You can come away willingly or I'll place all of you under arrest on suspicion of murder and take you down to headquarters."

"My office?" Chambrun suggested.

"All right with me," Hardy said. "Only we move now."

"I'll ask the Baroness," Helwig said. He started to close the door, but Hardy's broad shoulder pushed it back inward and we all went inside to the foyer.

"Don't ask her—tell her," Hardy said.

"It's all right, Marcus." Charmian's voice was clear and cool.

We trailed Hardy into the living room. Charmian was there, flanked by the Amazon, Madame Brunner. Both women were dressed in black, as though they might be on their way to a funeral service, but I swear there was no sign of hysteria, past or present. There was no suggestion that there had ever been tears. For the first time I began to think there was something inhuman about this whole collection of people.

"What is it you want to search for, Lieutenant?" Charmian asked.

Somehow she had changed. The youthful enthusiasm I'd sensed when she talked to me about her dinner party, the genuine shock I thought she'd felt at the news of Puzzi's death, had suggested a normal, attractive, vulnerable young woman. What I saw now was a cold, beautiful mask—a mask that hid the older, sophisticated, cruel woman who'd been described to us by Sam Culver in his tales about Bruno Wald and his own father. She was formidable and a little frightening. Someone incapable of feeling scares the hell out of me, I don't mind saying. I've run across a few others in my time at the Beaumont.

"Evidence of a crime," I heard Hardy say. I couldn't

take my eyes off Charmian.

"You think Heidi was killed here, in these rooms?"

"It's possible."

"It's absurd," Charmian said. "But if you've made up your mind to search, you will search."

"Yes, ma'am."

"Where do you suggest that we cool our heels while you paw over our belongings?" Charmian asked.

"Mr. Chambrun has suggested his office," Hardy said. "The time won't be wasted. I need formal statements from you and Mrs. Brunner."

Charmian turned her head ever so slightly toward Helwig. "He has the legal right to do this? It's an incredible invasion of privacy."

"I think we don't have much choice, Baroness," Helwig said. "He has the right to question us. He has not charged us with anything as yet, but he could and make it a great deal more uncomfortable for us."

"Then let's get it over with," Charmian said. She hadn't looked at me once, or Chambrun. "Will you get my mink jacket for me, Clara, and something for yourself. The hotel corridors may be drafty."

The Amazon disappeared into one of the bedrooms and returned with a three-quarter-length mink coat for Charmian and a black-cloth job for herself. Charmian slipped the fur coat over her shoulders and walked straight out into the hallway, looking neither right nor left.

"Where is Dr. Malinkov?" Hardy asked Helwig.

"In his bed—ill," Helwig said.

"Get him."

"But I tell you——"

"It's all right, Marcus. I'm here," a voice with a thick Slavic accent said, and Dr. Malinkov came through the connecting door to the next room. He was a fat, flabby little man with frightened black eyes. He was wrapped in a heavy overcoat with a sheepskin lining. He looked as though he was suffering from a malarial chill. The whites of his eyes had a yellowish tinge to them.

We trailed after Charmian to the elevators. It was as though she were in charge. We went down in the noiseless car to the second floor. In the outer office we found Miss Ruysdale, along with Sam Culver and a police detective named Dolan. Charmian stopped in the doorway when she saw Sam.

"You too?" she asked. "Do they think you may have murdered Heidi?"

Sam turned away. Evidently he had changed his mind about a walk. Chambrun had crossed to the door of his private office; he held it open for Charmian. She breezed past him into the luxurious room beyond. A few steps across the thick Oriental rug and she stopped.

"A genuine Picasso," she said. "How extraordinary." She looked around. "Where do you want me to sit? I don't see any bright lights. Don't you make murder suspects face the glare of bright lights?"

"One at a time," I heard Hardy say. I looked back and saw he was closing the door in the faces of Masters, the Amazon, and Dr. Malinkov. Helwig was allowed to come in. He was Charmian's lawyer.

"Choose whatever chair you like," Chambrun said to Charmian. "I suggest this one by my desk. May I get you some coffee—or a drink?"

"How civilized," Charmian said. She sat down in the big carved armchair and tossed the mink coat back from her shoulders. "I should be screaming demands at you to produce the killer of my friend Heidi. Instead, you're wasting priceless time arranging an inquisition for me. It would be laughable if it wasn't infuriating. Coffee, I think."

Chambrun moved over to the Turkish coffee-maker and came back with a demitasse, which he placed on the corner of his desk beside her chair.

"I don't think the lieutenant has an inquisition in mind, Baroness," he said, sitting down opposite her behind the desk. "Your legal adviser, Herr Helwig, has made it quite clear to us that he feels you may be in danger."

"Marcus is an old woman," she said, glancing at Helwig.

"Perhaps. But a very shrewd old woman," Chambrun said. His eyes were half hidden behind their heavy lids and the deep pouches. "We have reason to think that Heidi Brunner was killed in the hotel—possibly in your rooms —and carried, by way of the service elevator, to the place where she was found just off the street. The purpose in searching your rooms is to make certain whether or not it happened there. The reason for talking to you is in the hope of getting some sort of hint from you as to motive. Killing your dog would seem to be aimed at causing you pain. Killing your maid—I'm not so sure. It could be aimed at you. It could be part of some sort of internal combustion in your private world. We understand the girl hasn't ever been off the Island before; you haven't been away for twenty years. The others have been away rarely, if at all. The whole thing could be the result of some sort of spontaneous explosion. We have no way of guessing at it. We can only ask you. You must know every detail of every relationship on that private island of yours."

She looked at him coolly, but with a suggestion of respect for the questions he'd put to her.

Before she could answer we were interrupted by the noiseless entrance of Miss Ruysdale. She crossed over to Chambrun's desk and put a note and a small envelope down in front of him. He glanced at the note, then opened the envelope and took out of it a folded sheet of paper. His eyes widened. Then he held the sheet of paper out to Hardy. Hardy scowled at it and handed it back.

"This note," Chambrun said to Charmian, "was delivered to Sam Culver's letter box earlier this evening. He stopped at the desk a little while ago on his way out to take a walk, and it was handed to him." He shifted his glance. "Do they say who delivered it to the desk, Ruysdale?"

"Mr. Nevers is checking. It was handed in before he came on duty."

Chambrun looked back at the note. "This note, delivered to Sam Culver, says: *'If you value your life don't go to the Baroness Zetterstrom's dinner party.'* That's all it says. It's not signed."

"How perfectly ridiculous," Charmian said. "May I look at it?"

Chambrun leaned forward, holding the note so she could see it, but not releasing his hold on it.

"Do you recognize the handwriting, Baroness?"

"It's so precise, so careful, one guesses it's faked," Charmian said.

"My thought," Chambrun said. "Well, the day clerk will remember who handed it in." He put the note and envelope back on the desk in front of him. "In passing, I assume that in view of what's happened you won't proceed with plans for this party."

"Of course I will," Charmian said. "I won't be frightened out of doing something I want very much to do. I hope Sam hasn't taken this seriously."

"He's supposed to look at your mangled dog and your mangled friend and take this as a joke?" Chambrun asked.

"It's not a joke," she said. "It's a vicious, silly attempt to deny me a special pleasure. I am giving this party for Sam Culver. I owe him a party. He didn't know it at the time, but Sam was responsible for my coming up with everything on earth I've ever wanted."

"Conrad Zetterstrom?" Chambrun asked, a deadly quiet to his voice.

"What Conrad had to offer," Charmian said. "I propose to express my gratitude to Sam, my childhood friend, by throwing the biggest bash that's ever been given anywhere for him."

"Let's face reality, Baroness. There's been very little time for word to get around about this—this bash. Mark hasn't released anything to the press, have you, Mark?"

I shook my head. "Amato's the only person I've mentioned it to."

"And Shelda?" Chambrun asked.

"And Shelda." I thought I detected a faint gleam of amusement in his narrowed eyes.

"My point is, Baroness, that only your own little army of people know about it, plus three members of my staff who wouldn't dream of mentioning it without my permission. So this warning to Sam—where could it have come from except the nineteenth floor?"

Charmian sat very still and straight in the high-backed chair, her bright blue eyes fixed steadily on Chambrun.

"Let us ask some questions of ourselves, Baroness," Chambrun said. "Does any one of the people in your entourage have a reason for wishing you not to give this party?"

"Why on earth should any one?"

"No reason whatever," Helwig said, quietly.

"If Sam Culver refused your invitation, would you still go ahead with the party or would it become pointless?"

"It's to be for Sam!"

"Quite so. If, then, Sam refused to come, you'd probably give it up."

"I might have—before I saw that note. Now I'll give it, come hell or high water! I will not be pushed around, Mr. Chambrun."

"But the note, designed to have frightened Sam into refusing to come to the party, would seem like a reasonable way to get you to give it up."

"But why?"

Chambrun shrugged. "Perhaps nothing very sinister, Baroness. Your man Helwig there has told us he feels it is dangerous for you to be off the Island. Your late husband had many enemies, and now that he's dead you may become a target for these people. The killing of your dog has convinced Helwig you're in danger, and he thinks you should at once go back to the safety of your island. He knows you." Chambrun's mouth moved in a slow smile. "He knows you are stubborn, determined to have your own way. You've just made it quite clear. Now that you've seen the note you'll give the party 'come hell or high water.' That's stubborness, Baroness. Helwig knows it's a quality of yours. Perhaps he thought if he could frighten Sam into refusing the party invitation—a party which will take several days, perhaps a week, to prepare—you could be persuaded to leave here now, at once." He glanced at the stony-faced Helwig.

"You're suggesting I have to be managed, like a bad child?"

"I'm suggesting that you're not a coward, Baroness. When you're threatened, crossed, you hold your ground. That's not always wisdom, but it takes courage. Helwig has been described to me as a devious man. Could he have written the note?"

"Preposterous," she said. "Ask him."

"Masters? Can he have some urgent reason to want to get back to the Island?"

"What possible reason?"

"He's a killer, Baroness, a gun. It's silly for me to ask you how many times he used that gun, or other weapons, in your husband's service. You wouldn't tell me. But he too becomes a target. New York may be a very dangerous place for him to be."

"Masters goes where he's paid to go, and he's quite competent to take care of himself." Her eyes brightened. "He enjoys danger. He's bored when it's not just around the corner."

"Malinkov? The wide world is dangerous for him too, according to Helwig."

"Poor Malinkov," she said. "What he fears most is a sudden sharp pain in his chest, an unexpected thumping of his heart against his ribs, a cramp in his stomach—brought on, I should explain, by eating too much caviar with chopped onion. He's a quivering hypochondriac. He's terrified of death—in bed, in his dreams, at the breakfast table, in the bathroom. Study him. He seems to be concerned with time, constantly consulting his watch as if he were afraid of being late for an appointment. He's actually counting his pulse beats."

"The Island spells safety to him, then," Chambrun said. "He could have written the note in the hope you'd give up the party and go back there."

"Look at his fingers," Charmian said. "Arthritic. His writing is a hen-track scrawl. He couldn't produce that precise script if his life depended on it. And to save you time, Clara Brunner is German. She knows very little English. The note is an impossibility for her."

"Peter Wynn?"

"The one person who had no intention of returning to the Island. He and Heidi were to have been married in a few days—poor kid. No, Mr. Chambrun, whoever wrote that note, it wasn't one of my people. I'd stake my life on it."

"That's just what you may be doing," Chambrun said.

Charmian had moved a little memo pad around in front of her on Chambrun's desk. She'd taken a gold pen from her handbag and was scrawling something on the pad with a child's frowning concentration.

"That precise handwriting looks so easy to imitate," she said. "But it isn't." She tore the sheet off the pad, crumpled it into a little ball, and rolled it away along the polished top of the desk. "Well, Mr. Chambrun, do I spend the night here in your office?"

"You stay till Molloy's done upstairs," Hardy said.

. . .

It took Sergeant Molloy and the Homicide experts, assisted by Jerry Dodd, about two hours to go over the Zetterstrom rooms from top to bottom, picking up bags of dust in their little vacuum cleaners, examining every unexplained stain through their magnifying instruments, examining every piece of clothing in the closets and bureau drawers.

At the end of that time Molloy reported back in Chambrun's office that there wasn't the slightest sign of anything to indicate that Heidi Brunner had been killed in any one of the rooms and carried away from there.

Blood types had checked out at the police lab. The stains in the service area and elevator matched in type the dead girl's blood. It was a pretty solid guess at that point that Heidi had been killed in the service area or the elevator, taken down to the cellar level in the car, and carried out through the back alleys to the place where she'd been found.

"Clear trail all the way," Molloy said. "She bled like a stuck pig. She was gotten out into that service area—sweet-talked or at the point of a gun—clobbered, and cut up."

"If she bled so much," Hardy said, "seems impossible some of it didn't get on the killer."

"Nothing on any clothes we found. Masters' gun is clean, by the way. Not a trace of anything on the butt to indicate it was used on the dog or the girl."

"He had plenty of time to clean it up," Hardy said.

"Remarkable if there wasn't some small trace left, no matter how thorough he was," Molloy said. "But Dodd's come up with something interesting." He looked at Jerry.

"May be nothing," Jerry said. "You remember that pale-blue Carnaby Street outfit Peter Wynn was wearing when the Zetterstrom party arrived at the hotel? Well, it's missing. Nowhere in the apartment. He's wearing an ordinary business suit now, you know. There are three or four other mod outfits in his closet, but not the pale-blue one."

"What does he say about it?" Hardy asked.

"Doesn't know why it isn't there," Jerry said. "He says he changed out of it in the late afternoon or early evening, after the dog had been found. You remember, he told us he was free to go out then? I gather the Amazon acts as a sort of house-mother for all of them. Wynn says she may have sent the clothes to the cleaner."

"Easy to check," Chambrun said, from the depths of his desk chair.

"Not so easy," Jerry said. "Cleaning service closes at seven o'clock. Our man doesn't have a home phone. I went through the tailor shop downstairs. No sign of that blue frock coat. It could have come down in time to go out to the cleaning people before they shut up shop. Be morning before we can know for sure."

"So ask Madame Brunner," Chambrun said.

Charmian Zetterstrom and her people were all in the outer office waiting for permission to reoccupy their rooms. Hardy went to the door and asked Madame Brunner to come in. The tall, erect, hard-faced woman came in. Helwig was at her heels.

"Just Madame Brunner," Hardy said.

"You'll need me," Helwig said. "Clara can't answer your questions."

"I have no difficulty with German," Chambrun said.

"It isn't that," Helwig said. "She can't speak. I can manage a hand language with her."

"She's a mute?" Hardy asked.

"She can't speak," Helwig said, his face stony.

"Deaf, too?"

"No."

"They go together," Hardy said.

The Amazon stood looking straight ahead at the far wall during this exchange. If she heard, there was no sign of it.

"During World War II Clara Brunner was a nurse in the prison complex commanded by General Zetterstrom," Helwig said. "She was a beautiful girl. It was easy for her to make friends with the prisoners. They confided in her, and she carried bits of information back to the General. One day she reported on a planned escape. The prisoners were caught in the act and several of them executed. A couple of nights later when Clara was on duty the prisoners, who'd learned that she was the cause of their failure, seized her, and—and her tongue was cut out."

"My God!" Hardy whispered.

I saw Molloy take a handkerchief out of his pocket and wipe the sudden beads of sweat from his forehead.

"General Zetterstrom did what he could for her," Helwig said. "He took her into his household and eventually to the Island."

"What happened to the men who mutilated her?" Chambrun asked in a flat, dead-sounding voice.

"Gas chambers," Helwig said. The tip of his tongue touched his lips. "After being treated to the same thing that Clara had suffered. An eye for an eye—the General's code."

I remembered those words spoken by Charmian. I felt

cold sweat trickling down my back. The Amazon still stared at the far wall, expressionless.

"What is it you want to ask her?" Helwig said.

Hardy cleared his throat, as though it was difficult to speak. "A suit of Peter Wynn's clothes is missing," he said. His voice was husky. "We wondered if Madame Brunner had sent them to the cleaners."

Helwig glanced at the Amazon. She shook her head slowly from side to side.

"It consisted of red trousers and a pale-blue frock coat," Jerry Dodd said. "He changed out of them late in the day. Did Madame Brunner see them?"

Again the slow negative headshake.

"She has no idea where they could be? They're not in your rooms anywhere."

The woman's hands moved in some sort of quick sign language.

"Have you asked Peter?" Helwig translated.

"Of course," Jerry said. "He changed out of them late in the day. Left them on a chair in his room, he says, because they were going to need pressing. He thought Mrs. Brunner might have sent them out for him."

"She didn't," Helwig said. "Why are you concerned about them?"

Jerry's shrewd eyes were fixed on the Amazon. "We think they may have been stained with Heidi Brunner's blood."

The Amazon might not have heard for all the reaction she showed.

"You suspect Peter?" Helwig asked.

"Right now we're just interested in finding those clothes," Jerry said. "Thanks for your help."

"Can we go back to our rooms now?" Helwig asked.

Jerry glanced at Hardy. The Lieutenant shrugged. "Why not?" he said. "I'm putting a guard outside your doors, Mr. Helwig. None of you is to leave the hotel without my permission."

"It will be a relief to have some privacy again," Helwig said. "Shall we go, Clara?"

"One moment," Chambrun said.

The Amazon turned to look at him.

"The girl was your daughter, Madame Brunner. We've searched for a motive that involved the Baroness. It's possible she was killed to get back at you; that you were the object of a grim punishment."

"Absurd," Helwig said.

"You had guests on the Island—war criminals. Perhaps one of them—"

"We had no war criminals on the Island," Helwig said. "That was a pipe dream of the Wald brothers. The Greek police cleared us of all suspicion of that ridiculous charge."

Chambrun was silent for a moment and then he shrugged. "You may go," he said.

The Amazon turned, like someone in a trance, and walked stiffly out of the room.

A sound like a deflating balloon came from Molloy. "What the hell kind of people are these?" he asked no one in particular.

"The monsters who almost pinned us to the mat a generation ago," Chambrun said. He lifted his demitasse to his lips and put it down abruptly. It was obviously stone-cold. "Any report yet on who left that note for Sam Culver?" he asked.

"Negative," Jerry Dodd said. "Just one of those things. Along about five o'clock that cultural delegation to the U.N. from Thailand was checking in. There was a lot of confusion—interpreters—God knows what else. When Atterbury finally got them untangled and off to their quarters he noticed that note for Sam lying on the desk by the registration blotter. He hadn't seen who put it there. It didn't seem important and he just put it in Sam Culver's mailbox. You know Atterbury? He says he may be able to dredge it up 'out of his subconscious' later, but right now he has no memory of anyone putting the note there. He was surrounded by people jabbering a strange language at him. He was busy."

"Someone else is getting all the breaks at the moment," Chambrun said.

"You believe what you told the Baroness—that the note was meant to persuade Culver to refuse the invitation to her party so that she herself could be persuaded to go back to the Island?" Hardy asked.

"Not for a minute," Chambrun said.

"But why—?"

"I was content to let them all think I believed that," Chambrun said. He took a deep drag on his cigarette, his eyes narrowed. "We've been so concerned with facts—

bloodstains, where it all happened, a search for missing weapons, missing clothes—we haven't come to the point of considering a solid motive for the murder of the girl."

"None of them can be believed," Molloy said.

"Take the note at face value," Chambrun said. "It warns Sam Culver that his life is in danger, particularly if he attends the Baroness' party. Let's assume for a moment that Heidi Brunner wrote that note and slipped it onto the desk during the confusion Atterbury described. She could have been killed for having warned Sam and to keep her from telling him exactly what the danger is."

Hardy's lips pursed in a soft whistle.

"If the girl confided in anyone it would most likely have been Peter Wynn. They were in love, by all accounts."

"Who believes what anyone tells you?" Molloy said. "Wynn didn't mention any such thing when we talked to him. You'd think he would have if he cared about the girl."

"None of these people, from the Baroness on down the line, places a very high value on human life," Chambrun said. "Wynn may very well think it's safer to keep his mouth shut. Where is he?"

"My office in the lobby," Jerry Dodd said. "He was to stay there till I told him it was all right to go back to his room. I haven't told him."

"Get him up here," Chambrun said. "Meanwhile, I think it's time we talked to Sam."

Jerry went to the outer office to phone.

Sam looked old and beaten when he came in from Miss

Ruysdale's office. His hand was unsteady as he held a lighter to his cold pipe.

"I thought you should know about the note while you were talking to the others," he said to Chambrun.

"You better pour yourself a drink," Chambrun said, gesturing toward the sideboard.

"I'm past the point where a drink will do me any good," Sam said. He sat down in the big armchair recently occupied by Charmian. He shook his head slowly. "Even when she's gone you can smell her perfume," he said.

"What do you make of the note?" Chambrun asked.

"Kid stuff—except that there is death all around us," Sam said. "So why not mine, too?"

"Why would one of them want you dead?"

"Search me," Sam said. "Except that the Zetterstrom people play everything larger than life. Death for stealing an apple, or passing a small insult."

"You insulted anyone recently?"

"Who knows?" Sam said.

"I think you better tell us what you left out earlier," Chambrun said.

"Left out?" Sam sounded surprised.

"You came away from the Baroness white-hot. You needed a walk. You needed fresh air. Something happened there, before we interrupted about the dog, to turn you on, Sam. What was it?"

Sam sank deeper into his chair. "The Charmian Brown saga," he said. "It seems it may never end." He put his pipe down on Chambrun's desk as though he were reluctant to part with it. "I was intrigued when you brought me her message, Mark—that she wanted to see me, to apologize for having snubbed me on her arrival, and to invite me to some cockeyed party. I felt a strong impulse—curiosity, whatever—to see Charmian face to face. I wanted to discover what the years had done to her, or perhaps miraculously, what they had not done to her. Deep down in my subconscious I think there's always been a big black question mark. That moment of love-making with Charmian twenty years ago—had it really been solely to find out the truth about my father, or had I always had an insatiable man-woman hunger for her ever since the days when we played 'doctor' under the front porch? Had I punished her, driven her out of Hollywood, not so much to gain justice for my father, but to do something about my own guilt for having so much wanted the woman who'd betrayed the old man and driven him to suicide?" Sam gave Chambrun a crooked litttle smile. "Subsurface Sam, they call me."

"I can understand your wondering," Chambrun said.

Sam went on. "I was rather unpleasantly startled to discover, as I walked down the corridor toward 19-B that my heart was beating faster than normal. The old teen-age excitement.

"This girl Heidi answered the door. I was expected. I was ushered, without delay, into the living room where Charmian sat on that gold-brocaded love seat. You saw her in that yellow shift. Her smile was tentative, as if she were a little afraid of seeing me again. We were alone—I thought. Heidi had evaporated. I had no reason to suspect then that Helwig and Masters might be within earshot.

"I found I couldn't speak for a moment; my heart was thumping against my ribs. Her wide blue eyes, fixed intently on me, seemed to plead for something. My mouth was cotton-dry.

" 'Well, Charmian,' I heard myself say.

" 'Well, Sam?' It was the low, throaty voice I remembered so well, still young and vibrant.

"I felt myself getting on top of this silly emotional disturbance. But she was unbelievable. You've seen, Pierre. I'd been impressed by her appearance during those moments in the lobby, but then she was wearing the sable coat and hat, she had on the black glasses. She'd looked amazingly unchanged by the passing twenty years, but most of what would have been tell-tale exposures were hidden. Now she was without the glasses, and there were no crow's-feet at the corners of her eyes. The shift was scanty in terms of covering her exquisite figure—arms bare, long legs carelessly exposed. There was no flabbiness, no sag, no signs whatever of age."

"I can vouch for that," I said.

Sam's weary eyes turned my way. "Don't be had by the siren song, Mark," he said. "Well, anyway, I told her she was a miracle. She said she was glad I thought so, and asked me to sit down in the corner of the love seat opposite her. I did, and was instantly aware of her perfume—just as I was when I sat down in this chair. Not too heavy, deliciously subtle. I remembered it well from that night twenty years ago. I'm sure it's made specially for her. She invited me to have a drink and I refused.

" 'It's always been my theory,' she said, 'that drinking should only be done when all you want of the moment is the experience of being a little tight. It doesn't go with other sensations or pleasures.'

"She'd said something almost exactly like that on the night I'd found myself lying beside her in her mammoth Hollywood bed.

" 'Men are lucky,' she said. 'They age so attractively. You're handsomer and stronger looking, in the sense of character, than you were twenty years ago.'

"I found it difficult to keep this light, conversational ball bouncing. Her youthfulness, her total lack of change, were dazing.

" 'It's too bad you're so very rich,' I said.

" 'Oh?'

" 'You'll miss the satisfaction of making an enormous fortune on your own. If you could bottle and market the secret of your perpetual youth, Charmian, you'd have the women of the world at your feet.' It was a first-class inanity.

" 'I'm sorry that impresses you so much,' she said. 'Presently you'll begin to think about it—the massage, the lotions, the exercises, the magic of Dr. Malinkov. You'll stop believing it's real—which of course it isn't. Tell me about you, Sam.'

"I told her I'd made a lot of money in Hollywood. It had allowed me to do the kind of writing I really liked. I told her it had been a good life.

"'Women?' she asked.

"'Here and there.'

"'But no one permanent?'

"'No.'

"She laughed. 'Vanity is the scourge of womankind,' she said. 'I'd like to think it was because you really never got over me, Sam.'

"'Coming down the hall a few minutes ago I wondered about that myself.'

"'How sweet,' she said.

"Well, I told myself, here we come around to the brass ring again. Twenty years ago I knew her next move would have been to slip out of that yellow nothing, take me by the hand, and lead me to a huge circular bed surrounded by mirrors. Goddamn it, I found myself half hoping! But when it didn't instantly happen, a new absurdity occurred to me, an absurdity that turned me off but good. *This isn't Charmian, I thought. This is a stand-in, a double.*

"As if she'd been reading my mind, she said: 'I remember everything we said to each other that night, Sam, as if it had been recorded on tape. I wanted you for the man you were, Sam, and also for what you could do for me in Hollywood. Always greedy! Always ready to play both sides of the street was Charmian Brown. I knew you were going to ask me that question about your father, and I was determined not to be cheated out of having you by answering it too soon. Remember? You started to ask me several times and I wouldn't let you say it.'

"I remembered—too damned vividly; her fingers on my lips, that wonderful sensuous body pressed close to me. Oh, I remembered.

"'Then afterwards—so soon afterwards—you asked me,' Charmian said. 'You can't imagine how carefully I debated my answer to that question. If I told you your father was guilty you might run out on me because you couldn't bear the thought of sharing me with him. If I told you he was innocent you might run away, but you'd get over it and you might come back. I guessed wrong.'

"'Guessed! I couldn't believe my ears. I felt myself shaking from head to foot. 'What was the truth?' I asked her.

"She looked at me and her lips curled downward in an expression of slight disgust. 'The lecherous old goat was all over me that night, Sam. I screamed for help because I needed help.'

"My God, I thought, this is no double, no stand-in. This is Charmian Brown, who knows all the techniques of turning the knife in the wound until you cry out for mercy. A kaleidescope of horrors was in front of me: my father hanging from that pipe in the basement; Bruno Wald, reveling in an illicit pleasure and then caught in it like a rat in a trap; and God alone knew how many other faceless victims. Bitch, bitch, bitch! I'd never know the truth about my father now. She'd tell it to me one way today and another way tomorrow. She had me on a string like a yo-yo. What sweet revenge for her. Twenty years ago I'd driven her out of Hollywood, destroyed her chance for a career, and now she'd squared accounts with me. You ask if it can matter after all this time? Well, Goddamn it, it does matter! I heard her asking me, sweetly, if I'd come to her party, and I told myself, 'I will kill her!.' I felt better." Sam drew a deep breath. "And then you and Mark arrived to tell her about the dog."

"Why didn't you tell us this part of it when you first told us the story about your father?" Chambrun asked.

"Do you know, Pierre, I really did think about killing her." Sam laughed. "The impulse was so real I was already planning how to cover myself. I did go for a walk to think it all out. As I cooled out I realized, of course, that I couldn't kill her—that it wouldn't satisfy. On my way in through the lobby Nevers beckoned to me from the desk. There was that note. And while I was reading it, not quite believing what I read, a heavy hand rested on my shoulder and it was that Homicide dick named Dolan. I was wanted back up here."

"We come back to motive," Chambrun said, after a moment. He'd picked up the litttle ball of paper Charmian had left crumpled on his desk a couple of hours before. He tossed it up and caught it—tossed it up again. It was irritating to watch. "We have a nice motive for you, Sam, except that Charmian Zetterstrom is still very much alive. But what is the motive behind a possible plan to do you harm at the party?"

"Poison my soup," Sam said.

I found myself smiling as I thought of Amato's remarks about kangaroo tail soup.

"But why?" Chambrun said. "What you did happened

twenty years ago. She's had a fabulous life since then—money, power, a free hand to indulge all her peculiarities."

"She's like the elephant who never forgets," Sam said. "I grew up on stories about elephants who killed cruel handlers dozens of years after the fact. You don't cross Charmian Brown without paying for it."

"She's had her revenge, hasn't she?" Chambrun said, tossing the little ball of paper up and down. "She's stuck the knife in you a second time about your father. She's shrewd enough to know what that's done to you. 'If you value your life,' the note says. How far does she have to go to square accounts?"

"Right now I've got a murder that's already happened to bother me," Hardy said.

"Sam has reason to be concerned about himself," Chambrun said.

"So stay out of her way, Mr. Culver. You want protection, we'll give it to you," Hardy said.

Chambrun tossed the little ball of paper into the ashtray on his desk. He was frowning. "I find myself more concerned with preventing the next move in this game than cleaning up the mess behind us," he said.

"I think she may be the most evil woman on the face of the earth," Sam said, his voice unsteady. "Is there no way to stop her from killing people at will?"

"We'll stop her," Hardy said. "She's not on her island now."

"Let us pray," Chambrun said. . . .

3

Peter Wynn looked like a man in a trance when he was brought into Chambrun's office by Jerry Dodd. It was almost four in the morning. Wynn had been sitting in Jerry's office on the main floor for hours, under the watchful eye of Sergeant Dolan. He was haggard. He needed a shave. All the elegance and youthful bounce that had been his trademark when Shelda and I had talked with him in the Trapeze in the early evening was gone.

"You know what happened to Heidi?" he asked, looking from Chambrun to Hardy. "That big baboon downstairs wouldn't tell me a thing. And I've run out of cigarettes."

Chambrun slid the lacquer box that contained his Egyptian variety across the polished desk top. Wynn took one, lit it, and inhaled hungrily.

"We hope you can help us," Chambrun said.

"How, for Godsake?"

"The truth would be a useful commodity."

"What truth?"

"When we suggested to you that Masters might be responsible, you reacted hard and shut up like a clam," Hardy said.

"Masters is a machine, not a man," Wynn said. "You press a button, if you are Helwig or Charmian, and Masters goes into action. He's a gun, not a man. If Masters killed Heidi he did it because somebody pressed a button."

"Charmian?" Chambrun asked.

"Or Marcus," Wynn said. "He runs our world."

"You're not in your world now," Hardy said.

Wynn's smile was thin. "Persuade Marcus and Charmian of that," he said.

"Let me put our cards on the table, Mr. Wynn," Chambrun said. "What has happened here relates to what you call 'our world'—the Zetterstrom world, the Island world."

"The man in the lobby this afternoon wasn't from the Island," Wynn said.

"His brother was a part of that world. Do you know the story of Bruno Wald?"

"Naturally. He was drowned in a yachting accident—or so they believed. I understand he turned up ten years later, delirious, out of his head."

"You know the story he told?"

"Yes. Completely out of his head."

"That story doesn't frighten you?"

"Why should it?"

"Because aren't you in exactly the same position he was?" Chambrun asked. "The truth, Mr. Wynn. Weren't you hired to take care of the Baroness' sexual whims?"

"Good Lord, no!"

"Would you like to tell us how you happened to be on the Island—eighteen months, I understand?"

Wynn crushed out his cigarette and reached for another. "I've never had any money of my own," he said. "My talents are limited strictly to sports. I'm a good tennis player, a better than fair golfer, I play squash, I swim, I'm good with boats. I got along in my late teens and early twenties by being the ideal house guest. I dance well. I play several musical instruments, including a pretty good jazz piano. I made a business of making myself attractive at parties. I was on a yachting trip with some people from the south of France who got invited to the Island. The Island is something you wouldn't believe. There's everything there; fresh- and salt-water swimming pools, the sea itself, squash courts, tennis courts, a nine-hole golf course. Wish for something and it's there. The Baron didn't overlook anything to satisfy the slightest whim.

"The party I went with stayed for a week or ten days. I made myself popular by playing at the different sports. I'm a better than average bridge player. Made myself some pocket money that way. I ingratiated myself by playing tennis with Charmian, and with Heidi.

"When it came time for my party to leave, Helwig summoned me into his presence. He offered me a job, at an incredible wage. I would stay on the Island as a sort of director of sports, help entertain Charmian's guests, and act as an escort for her when she needed one."

"I thought she never left the Island," Hardy said.

"She didn't. But people came—often. There were endless dinners, and picnics, and balls. I was to be her partner at these wing-dings."

"No sex?"

"I wouldn't have minded," Wynn said, "but no sex. It was the cushiest job you can imagine for a man of my temperament and gifts. And Heidi? Well, I fell in love with her. Simple as that."

"You knew the Baron was her father?"

"I knew it—when things got serious."

"Serious?"

"When we talked of marriage," Wynn said. "That was a few months ago."

"Did you find you were a prisoner on the Island?" Chambrun asked.

Wynn frowned at the end of his cigarette. "You're thinking about Bruno Wald's wild story," he said. "Will you believe it if I tell you I never had reason to find out? I never wanted to leave the Island. I had no family to go back to, no real friends. I was perfectly content to stay there and I never suggested leaving."

"Haven't we had enough of this travelogue?" Hardy said.

"Let's get back to Masters," Chambrun said, ignoring Hardy's complaint. "When you were here before, I asked you if Masters was interested in Heidi. You did a take and said 'Oh, my God!' You left us thinking that he might have been."

Wynn didn't speak for a moment. His face had gone hard. There was a curious ambivalence in this young man. One minute he seemed weak and shallow; the next, there were signs of an unexpected strength.

"There's nothing simple about any of us on the Island," he said slowly. "I'm the easiest to understand, I guess. I'm lazy. I like luxury. I don't have any particular goal in life except the next day's pleasures. I—I've sold myself out all my life because it was easier to get what I enjoyed that way. But the others, God! It all goes back to Baron Zetterstrom. He must have been a monster."

"In spades," Chambrun said.

"Helwig and Clara and Masters all go back to a time when the Baron was some kind of prime sadist in the Nazi picture. None of them has a shred of conscience about those days. Most of what I know about it comes from Masters. He loves to talk about the tortures, the murders, the violence. He comes alive when he talks about the mutilations, like Clara's. He's described to me a hundred times what happened to the prisoners who'd worked over Clara." Wynn shuddered. "You'd have to hear him to believe that he's like a hungry man describing a gourmet dinner. He's a classic voyeur."

"What the hell is that?" Hardy asked.

"A peeping tom," Chambrun said, drily.

"I think he had my job—Charmian's escort—before I

came to the Island. He—he evidently had responsibilities that I don't have."

"Her love-life?"

"So he says. He's told me in detail what she's like in bed. And yet I could swear that in the eighteen months I've been a part of the scene there's been nothing between them."

"He resents you? Does he know that you're not involved in that aspect of the lady's life?"

"He teases me about it. Tells me what I'm missing."

"Had he turned to Heidi for his pleasures?"

"No! Heidi hated him; was afraid of him." Wynn reached for a fresh cigarette in the lacquer box. He didn't light it. "Heidi loved Charmian. They were friends, as though there weren't more than twenty years' difference in their ages. They were like two schoolgirls together. Heidi was convinced that someday Masters would do Charmian some harm."

"Because he'd been shoved out of the lady's bed?"

"Perhaps. When you asked me about him before, the thought crossed my mind that Heidi had caught him out in something. He wouldn't hesitate to kill if someone got in his way."

"Had Heidi confided in you what she feared?"

"No. It was very vague. A kind of premonition."

"What about the party Charmian is planning to give?" Chambrun leaned forward in his chair.

"The dinner for Mr. Culver?"

"Yes."

"What about it? Mr. Culver is an old friend." A tiny smile twisted Wynn's mouth. "I've heard the story. How he drove her out of Hollywood. Ironically, she fell into a pot of gold. Culver actually did her a favor. It's typical of Charmian's sense of humor that she'd give him a party to thank him for it, though he meant to do her harm."

Chambrun reached out and took from its envelope the note that had been left at the desk for Sam Culver. He showed it to Wynn. "*If you value your life don't go to the Baroness Zetterstroms's dinner party.*" Wynn stared at it, his eyes widened.

"Do you recognize that handwriting?" Chambrun asked.

"No."

"Is it Heidi's?"

"Good God, no."

"The Baroness'?"

"No. Of course it could be disguised, faked."

"It has occurred to us," Chambrun said, "that Heidi may have learned of some plan to kill Sam Culver; that she left this note at the desk to warn him; and that she was killed for meddling in the matter."

"Did she leave the note at the desk?"

"We don't know. Did she suggest to you that there was something about the planned party that worried her?"

"No. I can't remember that we ever talked about the party. Do you believe there is a plan to murder Mr. Culver?"

"It's easy to believe almost anything about your crowd, Mr. Wynn."

"About that fancy-dress suit of yours," Hardy said.

"I told you. I left my clothes on a chair in my room. I assume Clara took them to be cleaned and pressed."

"She says not."

"Then I don't know what happened to them. The hotel valet?"

"We're checking," Hardy said. "We think they may be stained with the girl's blood."

Wynn's mouth dropped open. "You think I—?"

"Like Chambrun said, it's easy to believe almost anything around here."

Wynn shook his head. It wasn't the action of a guilty man. He was brushing away the suggestion as an absurdity. "What about the man in the lobby—Stephen Wood?" he asked.

"We're trying to pick him up," Hardy said.

"He struck me as a dangerous psychotic," Wynn said. "He obviously believes the wild story his brother told him. He's crazy for revenge."

"But not against Heidi Brunner," Hardy said.

"Any of us on the Island," Wynn said. "If Heidi caught him snooping around—"

"I'd like to discuss one more thing with you, Mr. Wynn," Chambrun said. Stephen Wood didn't seem to interest him. "You've been involved with the Zetterstrom picture for eighteen months. How do you account for Charmian Zetterstrom?"

"Account for her?"

"Her youth. The failure of time to do anything to her physical appearance."

"It's a miracle," Wynn said. He shook his head. "Oh, she works at it. Careful diet, exercise, massage. God knows what else. And there's Dr. Malinkov. He's got some kind of magic, I guess. He was a plastic surgeon, you know. Heidi has mentioned a thousand tiny face-liftings. They don't wait for the signs of aging to appear. They keep pace with Nature, you might say."

"If there are repeated operations there must be days at a time when you don't see her."

"Right."

"Clara Brunner and Malinkov take care of her during those periods?"

"Yes. I mean, who else?"

"Heidi?"

"Oh, I think so. I mean we never discussed it much. It was a part of the routine on the Island that you just took for granted. Every three or four months Charmian would disappear into her wing of the house for several days. We knew Malinkov was doing his job."

"Being as close to her as you are you must notice the tiny changes, the tightening of her skin here and there."

Wynn laughed. "She's an artist with makeup. You can bet your life she wouldn't put in an appearance after one of her sessions with Malinkov until she could hide every trace of what he'd done for her."

"There is a rumor," Chambrun said, "that the Island was a safe harbor for German war criminals. What about that, Wynn?"

Wynn shook his head, slowly. "Many people visited the

island in my time," he said. "I was never aware that any of them were wanted."

Hardy made a growling noise. "We aren't getting anywhere with this," he said. "You're free to go back to your room, Mr. Wynn, but not to leave the hotel without my permission."

Wynn and Hardy left.

Chambrun sat at his desk, his heavy lids lowered. He had retrieved from his ashtray the little ball of paper which Charmian had crumpled; he began tossing it up and down again. I wasn't sure he knew I was still there, but he hadn't dismissed me so I waited. The first gray light of dawn was beginning to seep through the office windows.

It wasn't a normal time to have a drink, but I felt I needed one. I went over to the sideboard and poured myself a slug of Scotch in a four-ounce shot glass.

As I turned back toward the chair I'd been occupying, I saw that Chambrun had unrolled the little ball of paper and spread it out flat on his desk, evidently interested in Charmian's unsuccessful attempt to imitate the handwriting on the Culver note. He looked up at me slowly.

"Have a look," he said.

I walked over behind his chair and looked down over his shoulder. There were four words written on the wrinkled paper. They were in no way an imitation of the handwriting on the other note. The handwriting on the Culver note was small and precise. These four words were written boldly, hurriedly:

Please, please help me.

Part Three

1

Chambrun sat, motionless, staring at the scrawled plea for help on the desk in front of him.

It didn't make sense to me. "She was playing games as usual," I said.

"I wonder," Chambrun said. He picked up the phone on his desk and got Mrs. Kiley, the night chief operator on the hotel switchboard. "Good morning, Mrs. Kiley. Will you locate Lieutenant Hardy for me and ask him to join me on the nineteenth floor, please." He took an envelope from his desk drawer, put the crumpled note in it, and slipped it into the inside pocket of his Oxford-gray jacket. "Let's find out," he said.

He stood up, checked the contents of his silver cigarette case, refilled it from the lacquer box, and took off.

On the nineteenth floor we waited for Hardy. At the far end of the corridor one of the lieutenant's men stood watch, and grinned at us.

"If I ask to see her I'll be told she's asleep," Chambrun said. "I need Hardy's authority." He lit a cigarette, took a couple of drags on it, then put it out in one of the sand-filled brass containers by the elevator. I knew the signs of impatience.

Hardy finally appeared, looking harassed. "I think we've got this thing in the bag," he said. "We just picked up Stephen Wood. He was heading for the elevators to this floor. There are bloodstains on his coat sleeve. He doesn't know how they got there. The lab will check. If it's Heidi Brunner's blood, we're in. What's with you?"

Chambrun showed him the "Please, please—" note.

"So we ask her," Hardy said.

"Not quite so fast," Chambrun said. "If she wanted help we could give her, why didn't she ask us outright instead of this mumbo jumbo?"

"Don't ask me why she does anything," Hardy said.

"Unless it's a prank," Chambrun said, "she was afraid to ask with her own people within earshot."

"She's afraid of her own people? Helwig, Masters, the woman?"

"Unless it's a prank," Chambrun repeated.

"I don't get it," Hardy said.

"I don't get it either," Chambrun said. "But if we walk in and ask her in front of Herr Helwig and Masters, we're not helping. That's why I wanted you here. I suggest you tell her you need to ask her some further questions; then take her down to my office—without the others."

"Let's go," Hardy said.

It seemed to take forever for someone to answer our ring at 19-B. When the door opened a few inches, the inside chain-lock still in place, it was Helwig who looked out at us.

"Yes?" he said.

"I want to talk to the Baroness," Hardy said.

"My dear Lieutenant, the lady is asleep."

"Wake her up."

"This is nothing short of outrageous," Helwig said. "She's exhausted, emotionally and physically. Can't you wait until she's had a few hours' rest?"

"Sorry," Hardy said. "I'm dealing with a homicide, Mr. Helwig."

Helwig's eyes were flinty-gray. It took him a long time to make up his mind. "It would seem I have no choice," he said. He pulled the door to, released the chain, then opened it wide for us. He was fully dressed.

We followed him into the living room. Masters was there, sitting on the little gold love seat. He, too, was dressed. The men obviously hadn't been interested in bed. Lights burned on the wall brackets, but daylight was now streaming through the windows that overlooked the East River. Masters' eyes were narrowed, cold. He wasn't the relaxed, mildly amused man we'd questioned a few hours earlier. This, I told myself, was the professional gun on the alert.

"Will you ask Clara to call the Baroness," Helwig said.

Masters hesitated, his eyes questioning Helwig. Then he

shrugged and started out of the room.

"Tell her to get dressed," Hardy said. "I'm taking her somewhere else to question her."

Masters went out without acknowledging the order. Helwig stood very erect, a little tense, I thought.

"Surely this is unnecessary," he said to Hardy. "I can answer any questions that have to do with the Baroness, or the rest of us." He turned his head. "I appeal to you, Mr. Chambrun. This is completely uncivilized."

Chambrun might not have heard him. He was staring at the door through which Masters had gone. The silence set my nerves on edge. Then Clara Brunner appeared. She was wearing the same black dress she'd had on earlier in the evening. She gave Helwig some incomprehensible hand signals.

"Impossible," Helwig said.

Clara nodded, affirmatively.

"What is it?" Hardy asked.

"Clara tells me the Baroness is not in her room," Helwig said.

Masters had reappeared in the doorway. He was smiling a thin smile, as though he was suddenly enjoying himself.

"Then she's in some other room," Hardy said. "Get her."

Helwig looked at Clara. She shook her head, this time negative. She made sign language. Helwig moistened his lips.

"She seems to have gone out somewhere," he said.

"Your man in the hall," Chambrun said.

Hardy turned and went to the hall door; we heard him call to the cop who was stationed out there.

"It's been an exhausting and highly disturbing evening for the Baroness," Helwig said. "She may have felt the need for a little fresh air—a chance to walk about and collect her thoughts."

"Only she didn't," Hardy said, coming back into the room. "No one's left your rooms, Mr. Helwig, since you were all checked in by my man. I don't want any more crap from you. You produce her, or I'll go in and drag her out myself."

"She isn't here," Helwig said, in a flat voice.

"Okay. I'll remember you made it tough," Hardy said. He headed for the door to the inner rooms. Masters blocked the way, casual but not relaxed. He looked past Hardy at Helwig. I saw the gray man nod. Masters stepped aside, grinning.

Chambrun looked at Helwig. "We're wasting time," he said. "You don't know where she is, do you?"

"But I've only just heard—"

"I doubt it," Chambrun said. "You're fully dressed. So are Masters and Madame Brunner. You were about to start a search of your own for her. Right? What about Malinkov and Wynn? Are they dressing to join your search party?"

"I assure you, Mr. Chambrun—"

"Don't assure me," Chambrun said. He turned and walked through the door at the far end of the room, past Masters. I followed him. Masters grinned at me. I could smell an overpowering aroma of whiskey. The man was half loaded.

Charmian's bedroom was empty. The big double bed had been turned down, but it didn't appear to have been slept in. The bathroom, shelves loaded with creams and lotions, was empty. The second bedroom of the suite was untouched. No one was using it.

As we went through the connecting door to the next room we encountered Malinkov. The doctor was wheezing as he tried to pull on a pair of pants over long winter underwear.

"Are we to have no privacy at all?" he asked.

We caught up with Hardy in the next single room, which was obviously Clara's. The lieutenant had just finished looking in the large stand-up closet.

"Just in case she's hiding out on us," he muttered.

The next room was Peter Wynn's. The young man was pulling on his jacket as we walked in.

"They say Charmian's missing," he said. "Gone out somewhere."

"Mind if I look in your closet and bathroom?" Hardy asked, not waiting for an answer.

"Where would she go—and why?" Wynn asked.

Nobody bothered to answer him.

The final suite of rooms was Helwig's. No sign of Charmian there. Hardy and Chambrun faced each other.

"She's not anywhere in these rooms, that's for sure," the lieutenant said. "She didn't go out in the hall. What do you make of it? Fire-escape?"

"Nothing outside the building," Chambrun said. "Fire

stairs. She'd have to go out into the hall to reach them."

"And she didn't."

"Your man says."

"You suggesting—?"

"There's more cash floating around in this setup than you can imagine," Chambrun said. "The Baroness could meet any price. Let's talk to your man."

We went out into the hall from Helwig's suite, leaving the door on the latch. Hardy's man was a plainclothes cop named Salinger.

"Find her?" he asked, as we joined him in the hall.

"No," Hardy said.

"Well, she didn't come out this way," Salinger said. "I checked them all in when Molloy brought 'em back here. Two women, three men—and later a fourth man. Wynn. None of 'em tried to come out again."

"You didn't leave here for anything? Go to the john? Drink of water?"

"Not for ten seconds," Salinger said. He seemed completely undisturbed by the line of questioning.

"What's your price?" Hardy asked, his voice harsh.

"How's that?"

"I said, What's your price? How much did the lady pay you to look the other way?"

"For Godsake, Lieutenant!"

"Well, how much?"

"You must of had a rough night," Salinger said. His face had gone white with anger. "If I didn't know you better I'd hand you my badge and bust you one."

"All right. I had to ask," Hardy said.

Salinger took a wallet out of his pocket. "Take a look," he said. "And go through my pockets." He began turning his pockets inside out. There were the usuals; cigarettes, a lighter, some kind of cough drops, matches, keys, and about eleven dollars and change in money. "Maybe she gave me a promissory note I hid somewhere," Salinger said. He was trembling with rage.

"Okay, okay, I said I had to ask," Hardy said.

Salinger began replacing his belongings in his pockets, unmollified.

"*I* made the suggestion you'd been bought," Chambrun said.

"You and your fancy flea-bag of a hotel!" Salinger said.

"It had to be thought of," Chambrun said. "It's the only way she could get out, and she has gotten out."

"Maybe she's the Flying Nun," Salinger said.

"If you weren't bribed, Salinger, she has to be something like that," Chambrun said. "You're a cop. You know you didn't turn your back. How did she make it?"

"All I can say is, she didn't make it this way."

"Was there any kind of disturbance—an argument down the hall—a cute chambermaid? Seriously, if you were distracted for that ten seconds you mentioned she could have slipped around the corner of the hallway."

"There was nothing," Salinger said. "No one spoke to me. No one went in or out of any of these rooms or the ones on the other side of the hall."

"Keep watching close," Hardy said. "The people inside are getting restless."

We went back into Helwig's deserted suite, leaving the still simmering Salinger to stand watch in the hall.

"What do you make of it?" Hardy asked.

Chambrun stood staring at the east windows of the sitting room. The fingertips of his right hand seemed to be unconsciously stroking the pocket that held the "Please, please—" note.

"I believe him," Chambrun said.

"Then how did she get out?"

Chambrun walked over to the windows and opened one. He beckoned to us. I have no head for heights. Just looking down nineteen stories to the street makes my stomach churn. The few taxis and trucks moving in the early-morning traffic looked like toys.

"There is a ledge about two feet wide," Chambrun said. "If you can imagine her standing out there, you have also to imagine her turning a corner of the building; otherwise, she'd have had to come back into one of her own rooms. She'd have to gamble on finding an open window somewhere, presumably into an empty room, or someone would have sounded the alarm."

"What about empty rooms?"

"Check," Chambrun said to me, and I went to the phone to call Nevers at the front desk. "It's more likely that your perfectly honest Salinger was distracted by something he doesn't remember," I heard Chambrun saying.

Nevers reported one empty room on the nineteenth floor. It was all the way around on the south side of the building. It would have required something almost unbelievable in balance and courage for anyone to edge along the ledge, turn the corner of the building, and edge along another thirty yards to that empty room.

"If you assume she went this way," Chambrun said when I reported to him, "you have to ask yourself a question. If she got around the corner of the building and into a room, empty or occupied, why didn't she phone us for help?"

"If she made it," Hardy said. He was looking down at the street, his face set.

"There are no overhangs, no jut-outs," Chambrun said, matter-of-factly. "If she fell, it would have been straight down to the sidewalk. We'd have heard about it."

"So we put the screws on these other freaks," Hardy said.

"But carefully," Chambrun said. "I don't want them to know she asked for help. I'd like to hear their explanation for what's happened."

We walked through the connecting rooms to what was Charmian's sitting room. The Zetterstrom forces were gathered there—Helwig, Masters, Clara Brunner, the doctor, and Peter Wynn. You could smell tension.

"There's a very small chance she got out into the hall without being seen," Chambrun said to Helwig. "Very small. The other possibility is that she edged her way along the ledge outside those windows, around the corner of the building, and into a room on the south side."

A strange animal noise came from Clara Brunner. Her hands moved in frantic signs.

"Clara reminds me that the Baroness is terrified of heights," Helwig said. "She'd never in the world have tried anything so risky."

"What interests me most, Herr Helwig, is why she went at all—so secretly," Chambrun said. "You clearly don't know where she is. You were all dressed or dressing to start a search for her when we arrived. You haven't even tried to invent an explanation."

"We don't have an explanation," Helwig said.

"How did you discover she was missing?"

Helwig glanced at his white-gold wrist watch. "A little less than an hour ago," he said. "We had all gone to bed. It has been an exhausting stretch of time for all of us: the trip from London, and then the series of violences here; your endless questioning. The Baroness was worn down to a thin edge. I've never seen her so close to cracking. We were all worried about her. Clara helped her prepare for bed, made sure she had everything she needed." ·

Clara Brunner's hands spoke again, rapidly.

"Clara says the Baroness didn't actually get into bed in her presence," Helwig interpreted. "She was going to take a hot bath—to relax. About a half an hour later Clara heard a sound—as though something had fallen in the Baroness' room. It could have been a fall, or a door or window slamming. In any case, she got up out of her own bed, put on her robe, and went into the Baroness' room.

The Baroness wasn't there—or in the bathroom, or any of the other rooms. Clara woke me and the others and we all searched for her. She was gone."

"Clara prepared her for bed, you say. Was she undressed?"

The Amazon nodded, her hands working.

"Undressed and wearing a dressing gown," Helwig said. He hesitated. "But she evidently dressed again. A plain black dress is missing, and a small handbag, and a pair of black shoes."

"So she intended to go somewhere?"

"So it would seem."

"Unless she was forced to go against her will," Chambrun said.

"By whom?" Helwig asked, his voice sharpened. "None of us has left here. Your man in the hall will tell you that. And yet, somehow, she did get out of these rooms."

I've listened to a lot of tall stories in my time and I flatter myself I have an ear for them. I could have sworn that Helwig wasn't acting. He was as puzzled as we were.

Chambrun tapped a cigarette on the back of his silver case and then lit it. His eyes were narrow slits in their deep pouches.

"I know it's futile to ask you, Herr Helwig, why the Baroness should be afraid of you," he said.

"Afraid of us?" Helwig said. "You must be dreaming, Mr. Chambrun. We are the people she depends on for everything. Masters is paid to protect her. Each of us handles some part of her very complex affairs. We are the only people she can trust without question."

"Then why this secret flight?"

"It is incredible," Helwig said. "But she must be found, and found at once. There is a murderer at large whom you haven't caught. However she was lured away, or persuaded to go, she is obviously in very real danger. Instead of standing here playing guessing games you should have the whole police force searching for her—the hotel staff."

"And me," Masters said. He was smiling, but his eyes were as cold as two newly minted dimes. "I'm not staying penned-up in this place, Lieutenant. I'm going out to find her."

"You'll stay here till I tell you," Hardy said. He was at the phone. The horse was gone, to coin a cliché, but Hardy was very efficiently closing the barn doors. Police were instructed to cover every exit from the Beaumont, public and private. A floor-to-floor search was ordered, which, I might say, would take a whole day if it was thorough. But we all knew, without putting it into words, that Charmian Zetterstrom could be miles away from the Beaumont by now if that was her purpose. Once she had made it into the public areas of the hotel she could simply have walked out the front door onto Fifth Avenue unnoticed.

2

At four-thirty in the morning an army of cleaners takes over the public areas of the Beaumont: the lobby, the bars, the restaurants, the ballroom, the public johns. They are armed with vacuum cleaners, brass- and glass-polishing potions, electrically driven trash wagons, dusters on long poles for cleaning the elaborate chandeliers, buckets and mops. There is nothing so efficient as old-fashioned elbow grease, according to Chambrun.

At six o'clock this highly efficient army was still at it. They had been at it at the exact time that Charmian Zetterstrom must have vanished from her suite on the nineteenth floor. This crew is made up largely of older women, and women have an instinctive way of noticing other women, particularly attractive ones.

The man in charge of this army is one Chester Gobillot, and he's worked at his job for longer than the memory of man. He knows all his workers, their aches and pains, their family problems. They trust him.

"No one noticed a lady going out at around five o'clock," Chester told Chambrun.

We were going back into Chambrun's office, involved in what might be called a meeting of the General Staff. Nevers, the night clerk, was there, and Mike Maggio, the night bell captain; Jerry Dodd; Mrs. Kiley, the night chief operator; Jacques Fresney, the head chef in the kitchens on that shift; and of course the efficient Miss Ruysdale.

"No reason they should, particularly," Chambrun said. "But they might have."

Chester grinned. "It's the people coming in interests them most," he said. "Some of them are in pretty rough shape after a night on the town. I remember——"

"Another time, Chester," Chambrun said. Like Hardy, he was closing the barn doors a little late. But even without advance instructions hotel people have a special gift for noticing things. A chic-looking woman going out at five o'clock in the morning would be noticed, simply because it wasn't ordinary. The doorman would have noticed; Mike Maggio, if he'd been in the lobby, would have noticed; and so would Karl Nevers. Surely if Charmian had left by any of the nonpublic routes she would have called attention to herself. Monsieur Fresney and his kitchen crew would have remembered if she'd passed through their domain. It was just barely possible she could have left the hotel unnoticed, but it wasn't probable.

"I'm guessing that she's still somewhere in the hotel,"

Chambrun said. "If she is, I'm also guessing that she will try to get to me. She may be trying to avoid Hardy's cops. I want it made easy for her to get to me. If any of you spot her, bring her here without involving the police if you can." He turned to Mrs. Kiley. "I want all phone calls to the Zetterstrom rooms on the nineteenth floor monitored, Mrs. Kiley."

"There have been no calls, in or out, since the girl was murdered," Mrs. Kiley said. "I took it on myself to keep track."

"Good woman," Chambrun said. I knew that eliminated the possibility that someone from outside had called Charmian and persuaded her to slip away.

Chambrun turned to Mike Maggio. "Two things, Mike," he said. "Atterbury didn't notice who left that note for Sam Culver at the desk. It's possible he didn't notice because it was someone he wouldn't notice—someone who might logically be there—a bellboy, a waiter. Was a bellboy ever summoned to 19-B? Was any room service involved? Were any maids on the floor asked to deliver the note?"

"Check," Mike said.

"And the missing clothes of Peter Wynn's—red pants, blue frock coat. If they were bloodstained I wonder if we aren't wasting time waiting for the valet to show up. More likely in a trash can or at the bottom of one of the laundry chutes. Follow up."

"Will do," Mike said.

"I want to talk to you, Jerry. The rest of you get back

on the job. This woman's life may depend on your keeping your eyes peeled."

They trooped out, all but Jerry Dodd. "It might improve the state of the world if something bad did happen to the Baroness Zetterstrom," Jerry said, drily. "Personally I couldn't care less, except for the bad publicity for the hotel. I can't forget the stories Sam Culver told us. That woman deserves trouble."

"Sam Culver is what I want to talk to you about," Chambrun said. "That note suggested he would be in some kind of danger at the party the lady was planning. It's just possible, in view of what's happened and is happening, that his danger moment may be moved up in time. I'm going to call him and suggest to him that he come down here. He can use my dressing room if he needs to sleep." Chambrun nodded toward the door of the small room where he keeps extra changes of clothes. There was a comfortable bed there, planned to provide the great man with a place to take forty winks during a busy day, something he had never thought of doing in his entire life.

Sam Culver was evidently in a deep sleep. It took him some time to answer Chambrun's call, and even longer to make any sense out of the story of Charmian's disappearance. He finally agreed to come down to the office.

When Chambrun replaced the telephone receiver, the little red button on the base of the phone began to blink. There is a conference box on the desk and Chambrun switched it on so that Jerry and I could hear. Lieutenant Hardy's voice was actually cheerful.

"Stephen Wood killed the dog," he said. "He admits it. Right now he denies having attacked the girl, but we ought to have it out of him before long."

"Where are you?"

"Jerry Dodd's office," Hardy said. "Care to join the party?"

"I care," Chambrun said. . . .

Stephen Wood looked like a man burning up with a fever. His eyes were hot coals in their sockets. He was slumped in an armchair in Jerry Dodd's office back of the lobby desk. He was wearing slacks and a soiled white shirt, necktie loosened at the collar. There was no sign of a coat in the office. I remembered Hardy had mentioned blooodstains on the sleeve. The jacket was probably at the police lab.

Hardy's first words to us confirmed that. "Lab checked out the dog's blood on this character's coat," he said. "That cracked him."

Sergeant Molloy was standing just back of Wood's chair. I imagined he and Hardy had been conducting a pretty tough session with Wood.

Wood's story, repeated disjointedly for us, wasn't pleasant to hear. The man had difficulty talking above a whisper. It was probably a combination of fatigue and a bruised larynx from the blow Masters had struck him earlier in the day. He kept moistening his lips, which looked fever-cracked.

"I killed the dog," he whispered. "I killed him. But

that's all, before God!"

"We got all day," Hardy said, "in which to hear about the dead girl."

"I tell you I never laid eyes on her."

"About the dog," Chambrun said, in a faraway voice.

As he talked, Wood seemed to writhe in his chair, as though he were in some kind of physical pain. It came out of him in little short bursts. Seeing Charmian in the lobby when she'd arrived the day before had acted like an explosion inside him. All his pent-up hatred for everything Zetterstrom had boiled over. It hadn't been helped by Masters' brutal attack. Wood was burning up with anger. Complicating his anger was the stubborn conviction that the woman he'd confronted in the lobby was not the Baroness Zetterstrom.

"She couldn't be!" he said. "I stood closer to her than I am to any of you in this room. I tell you that woman couldn't be forty years old! It's impossible. But that's not all. She looked straight at me when I called her name and nothing happened. I tell you, nothing! I don't care how iron her control is, there would have been something—a flicker of her eyelids, a tightening of her mouth. There was absolutely nothing. *And I am my brother Bruno's identical twin!*"

"The police believe that the story your brother told you was some kind of fantasy," Chambrun said.

"I know," Wood said, turning from side to side in his chair. "I know it was the truth, but that doesn't matter. Suppose she was innocent of any harm done to my brother. Suppose she really believed Bruno died in a boating accident. The sight of his double standing a foot away from her had to produce a reaction. It didn't. I tell you, that woman who's posing as the Baroness Zetterstrom never laid eyes on Bruno or she'd have been shocked by the sight of me."

Chambrun was silent for a moment, and then he said, patiently: "About the dog, Mr. Wood."

Wood seemed to ramble. "After Bruno was murdered —because he *was* murdered—I spent all my time trying to dig out facts about Zetterstrom Island and this evil woman who'd tortured Bruno. There are almost no photographs in existence of the Island or of the people who live there. It was, I learned, a rule of the house. Guests were not allowed to bring cameras to the Island. The press was never welcome. But some pictures were taken—two years ago, when Bruno's story was being investigated. They were taken by the Athens police." Wood waved toward a table in the corner of the office. I saw a scrapbook there. "I got copies of those pictures through a friend of mine who had some political influence in Greece. There is one picture of the Baroness, caught when she wasn't aware of it. Look at it. I beg you to look at it."

The pictures in the scrapbook were mostly of the buildings on the Island. They were hard to believe. The main house was enormous, its architecture a combination of Parthenon-classic and the overblown Hollywood of the thirties. There were pictures of the swimming pools, the tennis courts, the elaborate boathouses. It had all cost more money than my simple mind could imagine.

And there was a picture of Charmian. I should say there were several pictures of Charmian, but all except one of them were studio stills taken during her brief stay in Hollywood more than twenty years earlier. This woman, posed in various degrees of undress, was certainly the woman I knew. But the one picture taken on the Island was something else again. It was a shock. The photographer had caught her standing on a broad terrace just outside the front door of Zetterstrom's mansion. She had on black glasses. She was leaning on a cane. The photographer must have been some distance away from his subject but a telescopic lens of some sort had brought the woman's face into sharp focus. It was a face with lines at the corners of the familiar mouth. She looked haggard. She looked more than forty.

"That," Wood said, in a shaking voice, "is the Baroness—not the woman upstairs."

I have to admit I was rocked back on my heels.

Wood told us that on the previous afternoon he'd gone back to his hotel, when we'd released him after Dr. Partridge had checked him out. He'd gone there to get this scrapbook. He'd brought it back to the Beaumont, his purpose being to compare this photograph of the Baroness, taken two years before, with the woman in 19-B. He'd heard rumors of special youth-preserving treatments and operations. He wanted to assure himself by a second look at Charmian that she couldn't possibly be the Baroness in his picture.

Wood told us he got back into the hotel without being noticed, so far as he knew. He'd heard Helwig tell Charmian her rooms were on the nineteenth floor, and he went up there, imagining that sooner or later Charmian would make an appearance and he'd have a second chance to look at her closely. He'd waited out in the hallway on nineteen, standing near the door to the service elevator in case he had to beat a hasty retreat.

"Then suddenly that nasty little poodle was facing me, yipping at me," Wood said. Sweat was running down his face. "I—I kicked at him to drive him away, to shut him up, and—and he sank his needle-sharp little teeth into the calf of my leg. Look, you can see for yourself." He pulled up his trouser leg and exposed the mark of the dog's bite.

"I—I went completely off my head," Wood said. "I grabbed the dog by the throat, lifted him up, shook him—cursing at him. He began caterwauling and I was certain someone would hear and come looking for him. I carried him out into the service area. He was still yipping. I smashed his head against the stone floor, over and over, until he was silent. I can't explain, but I was in a kind of frenzy. There was what looked like a cargo hook hanging there on the wall. They tell me now that it's used by your people to move big burlap bags of trash onto the service elevator. I took it and I ripped the body of that miserable little beast to pieces. I—I stood there, looking down at what I'd done, and all the rage oozed out of me. I couldn't believe I could have done such a thing. My legs started to buckle under me. Some instinct made me pick up the bloody remains and jam them down into a metal trash can there in the area. Then—then I literally ran."

Wood sat there, breathing hard.

"But you hung around, waiting for the next member of the Zetterstrom party to show, and when the Brunner girl came out, hours later, you gave her the same treatment," Hardy said.

"No! I went back to my hotel. You can check out on that."

"We are," Hardy said.

"I went up to my room. I had a few drinks."

"You didn't need them. You were half tight," Jerry Dodd said.

"I had them," Wood said. "I lay down on my bed, hoping I could get drunk enough to go to sleep. Somehow I had to wipe out the picture of my own monstrous behavior. I couldn't sleep. I turned on my bedside radio. Sometimes that helps. I must have dozed off, but I woke up in the middle of a newscast. They were talking about a girl who'd been murdered in an alley near the Beaumont. They identified her as a member of the Baroness' party —Heidi Brunner. And—and it seemed to be a duplication of what I'd done to that poor dog."

Sergeant Molloy's smile was twisted. "Maybe you're like your twin brother, Mr. Wood. Maybe you suffer from lapses of memory. Maybe you came back here to the Beaumont, murdered the girl, dragged her out in the alley, and went back to your place and conveniently forgot all about it."

Wood shook his head, wearily. "I didn't come back here till after I'd heard that newscast. Then—then I had to. I had to know what was going on here. I mean, the girl—killed just the way I'd killed the dog."

"While you were in a trance," Molloy said, his voice harsh.

"I don't think there's much point in trying to force a square peg into a round hole, Sergeant," Chambrun said. We all stared at him. He was thumbing through Wood's scrapbook. "It would be nice if we could wrap the whole thing up in one package, have some breakfast, and go to bed. There are too many things going on—things that I know don't involve Mr. Wood—for me to buy him in a one-package deal."

"Like what?" Molloy asked, his feelings ruffled.

"Like where is Charmian Zetterstrom? Like where are Peter Wynn's clothes? Like who delivered the warning note to Sam Culver at the main desk? Those things for a starter, Sergeant." Chambrun turned the pages of the scrapbook and bent down to have a closer look at the picture of Charmian, leaning on a cane, her face lined. "You're not the only one, Mr. Wood, who wondered about the Baroness. Your friend Sam Culver had a 'feeling' about it. But she convinced him. She remembers intimate details of things that happened twenty years ago, snatches of conversation that only Charmian Brown could have known."

"She could have learned them," Wood said.

"Learned them?"

"Like a history lesson—from the real Baroness," Wood said.

"And where, do you suggest, is the real Baroness?"

"Back on her Island, torturing some other poor devil like my brother Bruno!"

"That is, at least, an interesting theory," Chambrun said. "And *this* Charmian Zetterstrom, the one who is here, who is she? She is certainly a double for these earlier pictures of Charmian Brown—the Hollywood Charmian."

"God only knows!"

Chambrun's voice was thoughtful. "Would you say a daughter?" he asked. . . .

That early morning was the first time I'd ever seen Chambrun when he didn't look bandbox-fresh. He needed a shave. He kept touching his face with the tips of his fingers, as if he were reminding himself that he needed to find time for his razor.

We had gone back to his office. I was bursting with questions. Did he really believe the Charmian we knew and were trying to find was not the Baroness—the Charmian Brown who had been involved years ago with Sam Culver? Did he really believe she might be Charmian Brown's daughter? None of it made any sense.

Miss Ruysdale was at her desk in the outer office when we got there. The long night had done nothing to her perpetual chic.

"Thank you for staying about, Ruysdale," Chambrun said.

"Where else would I be?" she asked. "If you don't need me—?"

"Oh, I need you, Ruysdale. I always need you. My compliments to Monsieur Fresney in the kitchen, and I'd like my breakfast now instead of at the usual time. A half a cantaloupe, broiled lamb kidneys, an English muffin, not too brown, and American coffee. And a bottle of properly chilled Rhine wine." He glanced at me. "You'd better have something, Mark."

"Ham and eggs," I said, and saw him shudder.

"Then, Ruysdale, will you drag Dr. Partridge out of his beauty sleep and ask him to report here. Ask Lieutenant Hardy, who's in Jerry's office, to have Dr. Malinkov brought here. And finally, have someone find me an electric razor."

"Your own razor and other toilet articles are in your dressing room," Ruysdale said. "I put them out for you, knowing you'd need them."

"Quite right. But I don't want to disturb Sam."

Ruysdale's frown was a thin pencil line. "I don't follow."

"Sam Culver is sleeping in my dressing room, isn't he?"

"I haven't seen him," Ruysdale said.

Chambrun scowled. "He probably went to sleep again after I called him. Wake him and tell him he's to get down here at once."

His cruise toward the inner-office door was stopped by the arrival of Mike Maggio, the night bell captain.

"Got some dope for you, boss," Mike said.

"Come in, Mike," Chambrun said, and went into his private sanctum. I saw him go over to the Turkish coffee-maker. It was cold.

"Item one," Mike said. "I can tell you about the note. I checked out room service records. Tea was served in 19-B late yesterday afternoon. The waiter was a fellow named Ruiz, Puerto Rican. Been with us eight years. On a hunch I got his home phone and called him."

"And?"

"He served the tea—tea, cucumber sandwiches, small cakes for three. The three ladies. I assumed the Baroness, the big one, and the dead girl. Ruiz was told to come back in three quarters of an hour for the tea wagon. He did. Check signed. Nice tip. He took the wagon downstairs and when he picked up the used napkins to throw them in the soiled laundry hamper he saw this note. Envelope, slip of paper attached to it, plus a five-dollar bill. The slip of paper simply said, 'Please deliver this to the front desk.' He thought it was odd no one had mentioned it to him directly, but five bucks is five bucks. He delivered the note."

"All three women were there when he came back for the tea wagon?"

"I asked him," Mike said. "They were all three there."

Chambrun was silent for a moment, letting it sink in. There was no way to guess which one of the women might have left the warning note under a used napkin on the wagon. My best guess was the Brunner girl. Someone had found out about it afterward and knocked her off.

"Item two," Mike said.

"Yes?" Chambrun's eyes seemed to be closed.

"The empty room on the nineteenth floor," Mike said. "Where the Baroness might have come in if she tried tightrope-walking the ledge. The windows were locked on the inside."

"She could have locked them after she got inside," Chambrun said.

Mike shook his head. "Dust, undisturbed," he said. "Room been unoccupied since day before yesterday. You know how it is, boss. A few hours unattended and you got dust and soot on all flat surfaces in this town."

"If she got into an occupied room," Chambrun said, slowly, "she would explain her problem, whatever it is, and get to the phone. She would have called me."

"Not necessarily," I said.

"She asked me for help," Chambrun said. "Mike, I want the file cards on everybody occupying rooms on that side of the hall on nineteen."

"Right," Mike said. "There's item three."

"What is it?"

"The clothes. Wynn's clothes. They were at the bottom of the laundry chute, spattered with blood. Sergeant Dolan was with me when I found them. He took 'em."

"Thanks, Mike. Good job."

Mike beamed. Praise from Chambrun was the equivalent of the Distinguished Service Medal. "I'll have those file cards here in nothing flat," he said, and took off.

Chambrun sat silent, staring down at his desk blotter.

"How long are you going to hold out on me?" I said. He looked up. "Hold out?"

"You believe Wood may be right? Charmian isn't the Baroness?"

"It's possible," he said, slowly. "She certainly didn't show any recognition of Wood in the lobby when she arrived. And she passed by Sam as though he were a stranger—though she explained that, not unreasonably. But there was a moment when we went to tell her about the dog. Do you remember? When I asked her, she said she hadn't recognized Wood. Helwig stepped in and told her Stephen is Bruno Wald's twin. She acted surprised, as though she'd never heard of a twin, and never heard the story Bruno told Stephen just before he died. 'What story?' she said. 'You all seem to know it but me.'"

I remembered. Helwig had said something about keeping the Bruno Wald story from her, which he said was utterly false, because it would have distressed her.

"The Baroness we've had described to us—a voluptuary, a cold, unfeeling woman who enjoyed torturing Bruno Wald and probably others, wouldn't have needed to have her feelings spared. It's hard to believe they'd have felt it necessary. But," and Chambrun shrugged, "they could have."

"The picture in the scrapbook," I said.

"Interesting," Chambrun said. "She showed her age there. Walking with a cane, no less. Still beautiful, but not young. That's why I want to talk to Malinkov in front of Doc Partridge. I want him to describe his techniques.

Maybe she grows old, and is refurbished by his surgical gifts periodically. Maybe she falls apart from time to time and is put together again."

"You believe that?"

"I'll listen to Malinkov's explanation."

Ruysdale came into the office. "Sam Culver doesn't answer his phone," she said.

"Probably on his way down," Chambrun said. "Took his good time about it."

A moment or two later Dr. Partridge appeared, wearing an old-fashioned flannel bathrobe over a hastily pulled-on pair of pants. His white hair was askew.

"Don't tell me you've produced another body for me?" he said. "What are you running here, Pierre, a slaughterhouse?"

"I want your medical opinion on a miracle," Chambrun said. He brought the doctor up to date on the story of Charmian Zetterstrom, her amazingly youthful appearance, the rumor that this was the result of Malinkov's gifts as a plastic surgeon, plus other magic of diet, massage, exercise, and makeup. "Is it possible, Doctor?"

"You could be fooled at a distance," the doctor said. "Let me see this woman up close and I'll tell you."

"I wish I could," Chambrun said. "She's out of circulation for the moment."

Ruysdale then ushered Sergeant Dolan into the room, bringing with him a reluctant Malinkov. The fat man was wheezing and sweating, his face the color of bread dough.

"I'm not well," he said, between chattering teeth. "I

should be in bed. I have a chill."

"This is Dr. Partridge," Chambrun said in a dry, hard voice. "He can prescribe for you if it gets serious. Please sit down, Dr. Malinkov."

"There's nothing I can tell you about Charmian's disappearance," Malinkov said. "I was asleep when Helwig discovered she was gone. I know nothing about it."

"I don't want to ask you about it," Chambrun said. "I want to talk to you about her as a medical case."

Malinkov's legs seemed to buckle. He almost crawled into the armchair by Chambrun's desk. He sat there, chewing on the knuckles of his clenched right fist.

"The Baroness is something of a miracle," Chambrun said. "From all accounts, your miracle, Dr. Malinkov. We know her to be forty-one or -two years old, yet she looks like a girl of twenty. We've been told that every two or three months she goes into retirement, that you do whatever it is you do, and age is miraculously defeated. Dr. Partridge and I are anxious to know just how you manage it."

Malinkov's mouth opened and closed like a beached fish. "It is very complicated," he said, his thick accent growing thicker. "It would be beyond the comprehension of a layman."

"Dr. Partridge isn't a layman," Chambrun said. "That's why I asked him to be here."

"I am a plastic surgeon," Malinkov said. He spread his hands as though that was all that needed to be said.

"Tell us how the Baroness happened to come under

173

your care," Chambrun said.

Malinkov shivered. "I was an old friend and associate of the Baron's," he said.

"You performed so-called experiments for him on Allied prisoners in World War II," Chambrun said, his eyes glittering.

"Yes. Then I came to this country—to help your doctors with the war-wounded—the mutilated. I can show you letters of gratitude from your government."

"I'm not questioning that, Doctor. About the Baroness, please."

"I—I had a letter from the Baron asking me to join his little community on Zetterstrom Island. I was obligated to him. I went."

"You would also be safer there," Chambrun said. "There were people who didn't appreciate the value of your wartime experiments for the Baron."

"Yes. That is true. The picture of things had changed."

"No more master race," Chambrun said. "So you went to the Island. I suggest you were needed on the Island. The Baron's war-criminal friends needed a change of face. You help to send these men out into the world, safe from prosecution."

"No, no!" Malinkov cried out. "Nothing like that. There were never any war criminals. I swear it."

"Then why did the Baron need you?"

"It was quickly explained to me why the Baron wanted me there. Charmian was afraid of growing old. It was not unnatural. She was so very beautiful—and there were beginning to be signs. She was then thirty, very active. No matter how carefully one conditions oneself with exercise, with diet, with massage—there begin to be signs."

"We have all seen those signs in the mirror," Chambrun said.

"I—I did what I could for her." The fat man turned to where Doc Partridge sat in the shadows. His smile was sickly. "You know how it is, Doctor. A little tuck in the skin here, a tightening there, a pulling back in another place. It can be done, a little at a time, without leaving scars." He looked back at Chambrun and shrugged.

"And so you stayed on, and you repeated this process every few months—the little tucks, and tightenings, and pullbacks?"

"Yes."

"And the result after ten years of this is the lovely, very young-looking woman who arrived here yesterday?"

"I flatter myself it has been most effective," Malinkov said.

"Bushwa!" Doc Partridge said. He comes from a much younger generation than mine.

"I beg your pardon?" Malinkov said.

"Poppycock!" Doc said. "Ten years of pulling and tugging and you'd have skin pulled over bones like a drumhead. You might hide wrinkles, but her skin would look like the seat of a saddle."

"I found my curiosity stimulated, Dr. Malinkov, by a photograph I've just seen," Chambrun said. "It was taken of the Baroness about two years ago, at the time of the second investigation into the death of Bruno Wald."

"Impossible," Malinkov said, sharply. "The Baroness never allowed her picture to be taken. Cameras were not allowed on the Island. Even those of us who lived there were not allowed cameras."

"This picture was taken by the Greek police," Chambrun said. "The Baroness was not aware that she was being photographed. She was leaning on a cane, Doctor, and she looked her age."

I thought Malinkov was going to dissolve in his chair like an overheated butterball. "I—I remember the time of the inquiry," he said. "I—the Baroness had sprained an ankle playing tennis. That explains the cane."

"But not the lines in her face, Doctor."

"I remember," Malinkov said. A little drool of saliva ran down his chins. "The inquiry came at a most awkward time. The Baroness was—was in the middle of one of her treatment periods. They insisted on seeing her. She was outraged."

"You took out the tucks and everything sagged?" Doc Partridge asked, in a voice of outrage.

"It—it was not a good time for her to be seen."

Chambrun sat very still, staring at the fat man. "When did the Baroness die?" he asked, quietly.

I thought Malinkov was going to have a stroke, then and there. His doughy complexion turned gray. One corner of his mouth sagged. Then he seemed to make a massive effort to pull himself together.

"You have found her? She is dead?" he whispered.

"I think you know very well what I'm asking you, Doctor. I'm not talking about the girl who came here with you yesterday and has since disappeared. I'm talking about the Baroness. The girl, I assume, is the daughter. The likeness is too striking to have been stumbled on by coincidence."

Malinkov's whole body shook. "You are quite mad," he said. "The Baroness—the woman you have seen and talked to—is Charmian Zetterstrom."

"I believe you," Chambrun said.

The silent Sergeant Dolan, Doc, and I exchanged glances.

"She is Charmian Zetterstrom," Chambrun said, "but she was never Charmian Brown. She is the daughter of the Baron and Charmian Brown."

"An absurdity!" Malinkov's voice was hollow. "I have known her, she has been my patient, for ten years."

Chambrun took a long time to remove a cigarette from his case and light it.

"I don't know the exact details of your personal problems, Dr. Malinkov," he said. "I know that you live in fear of your life. I know that you, like all the Baron's close associates, are haunted by enemies. I suspect that you stay with Herr Helwig, do what he tells you to do, partly because he knows too much about you, and partly because he is willing to protect you so long as you dance to his tune. You are now faced with a crisis of sorts. You're all playing some kind of game that's gone sour. I know that the Baroness you've presented to the public is a fraud.

177

There is a murder which leads straight to your doors. There are threats against other people." Chambrun took a deep drag on his cigarette. "I think you should consider very carefully, Doctor, whether it would be safer for you to accept an offer of help from us in return for information, for truth, or to go down with what is certainly a sinking ship."

Malinkov stared at him, his lips trembling, a hand raised vaguely to hide his faltering control. He seemed to shrink inside his clothes.

"You—you have invented an unreality," he said. "There is only one Baroness. I do not know what has happened to her, but I pray we find her quickly."

"Why did you all leave the Island, where you were safe?"

"The Baroness had not been away from the Island for more than twenty years. When the Baron died she was free to go where she wanted, do what she wanted. She is a young, attractive woman with a great fortune. She wanted to get back into the world when she had the chance."

"But she waited for two years after the Baron died."

"That was when the inclination to travel seized her," Malinkov said.

"I suggest that it took them nearly two years to school the daughter into taking her mother's place in public."

"No!"

Chambrun put out his cigarette, suddenly impatient. "I'm not sorry for you, Doctor. You've made your own bed and you choose to lie in it. I am sorry for Charmian

Zetterstrom, who is obviously in very great danger with no way to help herself. You and the others have brought her here to carry out some scheme. She has balked at it and is running for her life. God help her if we don't find her first. And God help you, Doctor, if we fail. I shall take a personal pleasure in acting for all the people who want to see you and your friends and Zetterstrom Island wiped off the face of the earth. Take him away, Sergeant."

Malinkov seemed incapable of getting up from his chair. Dolan had to take him under the arm and literally drag him to his feet.

"Would you believe it?" Dolan said, steadying the doctor on his rubbery legs. "Salinger was so sore at your suspecting him he walked off the job."

Chambrun's head jerked up. "Who replaced him?"

"No one yet," Dolan said. "I mean—he wasn't there when I went to get this guy for you. I'll report to Hardy when I get this one back."

"You bloody idiot!" Chambrun said. He was on his feet. "Who did you see in 19-B when you went to get Dr. Malinkov?"

"The woman, the gigolo, the doctor," Dolan said. "The other two were somewhere else in the suite, I guess."

"You guess!" Chambrun moved so fast we were all caught off guard. I traipsed after him into the outer office. He gave a crisp order to Miss Ruysdale. "Call Hardy. Tell him Salinger isn't at his post on nineteen. Tell him I think Helwig and Masters are on the loose somewhere. I'm on my way up."

"Right," Ruysdale said, reaching for her phone.

"And tell Jerry to spread a general alarm for Sam Culver. It can't have taken Sam this long to get here."

3

The daytime life of the hotel was beginning to revolve. Maids were visible in the hallways. Guests were riding the elevators on the way to breakfast in one of the restaurants. Everyday functions were being carried out with their usual efficiency. In another hour, I thought, as I followed Chambrun to the elevators, Shelda would show up at our office, sore at me for not having reported to her during the night about what was going on.

Chambrun had obviously worked out a portion of the puzzle, but I was way behind him—a little too breathless to do any solid putting together myself. He was as angry as I'd ever seen him as we were whisked up to the nineteenth floor in an elevator that ignored signals from the in-between floors.

On nineteen everything was quiet. There was no one watching the corridor outside the Zetterstrom rooms. Chambrun put his finger on the bell of 19-B and held it there. It was opened almost at once by Peter Wynn.

"Oh," he said. "Come in." He looked exhausted, yet tense.

Clara Brunner, sitting bolt upright in a straight-backed chair, was the only other occupant of the sitting room.

"Where are Helwig and Masters?" Chambrun asked Wynn, who followed us into the room.

"They went out somewhere," Wynn said.

"You don't know where they were going?"

"To look for Charmian," Wynn said.

"There was a man stationed in the hall to keep them from going anywhere," Chambrun said. "How did they get past him?"

"I don't know," Wynn said. "They just went out. I suppose they persuaded him they had a right to look for Charmian."

"They had no such right. How long ago did they leave?"

Wynn shrugged. "Forty-five minutes—an hour."

"Did they have any idea where to look for the girl?"

"Girl?"

"Stop playing games," Chambrun said harshly. "I know and you know that the missing girl is not the Baroness Zetterstrom."

A strange mumbling sound came out of the tongueless hole in Clara Brunner's bony face. Her hands fluttered helplessly. None of us could read what she was trying to say.

Wynn ran a hand over his long, red hair. "I saw no harm in it," he said.

"In the substitution of daughter for mother?"

Wynn nodded.

"When did the Baroness die?"

Again that ghoulish moaning sound from Clara Brunner. She was protesting to Wynn with her hands.

"I don't know what's going on here," Wynn said, in a tired voice. He glanced at the Amazon. "I have to think of myself, Clara."

The protest from the woman was an animal sound.

"The Baroness died before my first visit to the Island," Peter said. "The yachting party I was with—I told you about them—had been invited by the Baroness. But when we arrived, we were told by Helwig that the Baroness was ill, couldn't see anyone. We stayed for some days, waiting for the Baroness to come out and join the party. She never did. My friends decided to move on, and it was then that Helwig offered me a job. I accepted.

"As soon as my friends were gone, Helwig told me the truth. The Baroness had died about a week before. I got the impression it had been an incurable cancer. She is buried there on the Island. At least, there is a grave marked with her name. I was then told that my job was to instruct the Baroness' daughter in sports—teach her tennis, and golf, and squash racquets, games at which the Baroness had been expert." Wynn smiled. "It was about as pleasant a job as you can imagine. Charmian Zetterstrom—she was named after her mother, I gather—was a charming, effervescent, unspoiled kid. There were two daughters, you understand."

"Two daughters of the Baron—but not both by the Baroness," Chambrun said, glancing at the Amazon. Again there were those horrible, protesting mumbles from the woman.

Wynn shook his head. "They are—were—both Charmian Brown's children," he said. "I got it in bits and pieces from Masters. The girls were born a year apart, right after Charmian Brown married Baron Zetterstrom."

Chambrun glanced at the Amazon. "That would explain why Madame Brunner was able to take the murder of Heidi with such stolid fortitude. She wasn't your daughter, madame."

Clara Brunner's face had gone stone-hard.

"I gather children didn't fit into the scheme of things on the Island," Wynn said. A nerve twitched in his cheek. "If the Bruno Wald story is true—well, it's understandable. The two girls were shipped off to some sort of convent on the Greek mainland, where they were raised. It's my understanding neither of them ever came back to the Island until about six months before the Baroness died. They had been taught none of the things that went with the Island life, the sports and all that. That's why I was hired."

"The two girls inherited the Zetterstrom fortune?"

"It's my understanding that only Charmian inherited. Heidi was left out for some reason. I was told this when I made it clear I wanted to marry her. Charmian was all for the marriage. She made it clear Heidi and I'd never have to worry about money."

"Can we get to Charmian's impersonation of her mother?"

"It happened for the first time about six months after I'd been on the job. Some people who had been friends of the Baroness turned up unexpectedly at the Island. They came ashore. Charmian and I were on one of the tennis courts. She had never laid eyes on any of these people. Suddenly they crowded around her, embracing her, kissing her, telling her 'how wonderful she looked' and saying what an old genius Malinkov was. They quite obviously took her for the Baroness. Charmian was amused by it. She played it to the hilt without batting an eyelash. When the people went on to the house she laughed and laughed. What fun it would be, she said, to carry it off for as long as possible. I was sent on ahead to warn Helwig and the rest of the household. There didn't seem any harm in it. It was a big joke so far as I was concerned.

"There was one man in the group who must have been something more than a casual acquaintance of the Baroness. He obviously hated my guts. He made quite a few snide remarks about Charmian having resorted to 'robbing the cradle.' She played it magnificently, pretending to be romantically attached to me. It was still a big joke, and she carried it out down to the last moment when she waved good-bye to them from the dock. We laughed ourselves sick over the whole adventure for days.

"Then, about a month later, Helwig came to me one day. Some former business associates of the Baron were coming to the Island. It had to do with some complex money matters, he told me. These men who were coming didn't know that the Baroness had died. Helwig said he had persuaded Charmian to play the part again. The business at hand would be better handled if the men thought they were dealing with the Baroness, a cool, hard-headed operator, rather than with an inexperienced child."

"So she carried it off for a second time," Chambrun said.

"And a third, and a fourth," Wynn said. "Somehow, though, it had stopped amusing her. She seemed to change, to become moody. There were long, dark silences. Heidi and I were worried about her, but she never would tell us what was bothering her.

"Finally, a few weeks ago, we were told by Helwig that we would all make a trip to America. I was delighted. It seemed like the perfect time for Heidi and me to break away from our small little world. Charmian agreed. But she seemed curiously intense and depressed about the trip. I thought I knew why, a few days before we left. We were told by Helwig that Charmian would play the role of the Baroness while we were away from the Island. I assumed it had ceased to be fun for her. I didn't understand why she'd agreed to do it, but neither she nor anyone else explained it to me. Heidi was in the dark about it, too. We could only guess it had to do with business matters again." Wynn moistened his lips. "That's the whole story, Mr. Chambrun. I don't know what's going on. I can only guess that Heidi's murder has something to do with it, and so help me God, when I find out for sure—"

"You'd better leave it to the police," Chambrun said. "There's been no talk about Charmian's disappearance that could give you any kind of hint as to what's cooking?"

Wynn shook his head. "I can only tell you Helwig and Masters and the others are badly upset about it. They don't know when or how she got out of these rooms. Is there any way I can help?"

"When this lady reports to them how much you've told me you may be safer somewhere else. I'll have someone take you down to my office and we'll have a policeman stand guard there."

The doorbell rang and Chambrun signaled me to answer it. It was Jerry Dodd.

"Culver changed his mind," Jerry told Chambrun.

"What do you mean?"

"He decided not to come down to your office. He's sick of the whole thing, he says. He's decided to stay in his own place. I've got to admit he looks half dead for want of sleep."

Chambrun muttered softly under his breath. Then he instructed Jerry to take Wynn down to his office and have a cop placed on guard there. He turned to me. "Go up and talk to Sam," he said. "Make it clear to him that I think he may be in real danger. I want him to be somewhere he can be watched. My office is the place. We haven't got enough men to have every room in the hotel guarded." He turned back to Jerry. "I asked Mike Maggio to get me the file cards on everyone on this nineteenth floor. Would you be good enough to find out what kind of drag-ass he's playing."

Jerry grinned. "If you'd stay in one place for five minutes—"

I went up to the twenty-fifth floor, where Sam Culver has his cooperative apartment. I was feeling pretty thoroughly pooped-out myself by now. I rang Sam's doorbell three or four times before he opened the door to the width permitted by the chain-lock and looked out. Jerry was right. He looked like death. But I wondered why a man so anxious for sleep was fully dressed.

"Go away," he said.

"I am the bearer of a very insistent message from the boss," I said.

"Tell him to go peddle his papers," Sam said. "Let me alone, will you, Mark?"

"You were warned," I said. "We think it was probably by Charmian. She's disappeared and her two prize bully boys are loose somewhere. Chambrun thinks you may be a target of some sort. He wants you protected. Incidentally, your instinct was right. It's not Charmian Brown you're involved with. There's no Ponce de Leon mystery. This Charmian is her daughter. Till we can untangle it Chambrun doesn't think you're safe."

Sam's face turned stone-hard. He was silent for as long as twenty seconds. Then he said: "You might as well come in."

He closed the door enough to unhook the chain, then pulled it open. I walked in, wondering if he had any coffee brewing. The door closed behind me.

"I'm sorry, Mark," Sam said. "I tried to get you to go away."

I turned. Masters was leaning against the door, smiling at me. He had a gun in his hand. It wasn't pointed at me but he was caressing it, and I had a feeling he was split-second ready. I heard a movement behind me and turned again. Herr Helwig was standing in the bedroom door across the living room.

Masters chuckled. "Well, now we have a fourth for a couple of rubbers of bridge," he said. . . .

I guess almost everyone has had a moment in his life when he thinks, Here it is! Death. You step off the curb and see a speeding taxi coming down on you ten feet away; you have a violent cramp when you're swimming a hundred yards from shore; you're in a skidding car. These moments last only an instant because you get out of them. If you don't, you're dead and you stop worrying.

I had that sick feeling as I stood there, looking first at Masters and then at Helwig. They were both pretty damned frightening. Nothing, I told myself, would turn the gray man, Helwig, from whatever his course might be. A human life meant nothing to him. He had been trained under Baron Zetterstrom. Masters was even more scary to me. Pulling that trigger would be a kind of sport for him. He would actually enjoy it.

"Where are the cards?" I said, trying to sound flip and casual.

"You'd better sit down, Mr. Haskell," Helwig said.

"What's the game—if it isn't bridge?" I asked. Boy, was I playing the dime-novel hero!

"For some reason they think Charmian may show up here," Sam said. He walked over to his desk and took a pipe from the cherry-wood rack. He began to fill it from a porcelain jar.

"To tell you what they have cooked up for you?" I asked. "Is that it, Helwig?"

"He's a clever kid," Masters said.

"The situation borders on the absurd," Helwig said. "The police, bumbling as usual. Your pouter-pigeon Chambrun, imagining himself to be some sort of mastermind detective out of a storybook. Meanwhile, the Baroness is in danger, and we, her trusted friends, are denied the right to look for her or protect her."

"You mean the Baroness' daughter," I said. "You might as well know Chambrun got the whole pitch from Peter Wynn."

"Very well—Charmian Zetterstrom, the Baroness' daughter," Helwig said. "She is still our responsibility. She still depends on us."

"Then why did she run away from you?" I asked.

"A question I'm most interested to have answered," Helwig said. "It occurred to us that Mr. Culver or the man who calls himself Wood had persuaded her to leave our rooms. We came here to look for her. We think, since she isn't here, that she will almost certainly come here. Mr. Culver is the only friend, beside ourselves, she has in this part of the world. She wouldn't run to Stephen Wood.

He's obviously dangerous."

"Why don't you stop playing games with us?" I said. I had nothing to lose that I could see. "You want to find her before the cops do, because she knows one of you killed Heidi and she's ready to talk."

"I told you he was a clever, clever kid," Masters said.

"There's obviously no point in discussing this with you, Mr. Haskell," Helwig said. "So just sit down and wait."

"You got any coffee?" I asked Sam.

He gestured with his pipestem toward the kitchenette. "Electric percolator," he said.

"A cup of coffee against the rules?" I asked Masters. After all, he had the gun.

"Help yourself," he said, grinning at me. I had the unpleasant feeling he was like a gourmet looking at a magnificent dinner. I was the dinner.

I went out into the pantry and poured myself coffee in a white china mug. I knew the floor plan of these apartments well enough to know there was no exit from the kitchenette. I carried the coffee back into the living room. Helwig had disappeared into the bedroom. Masters lolled against the front door, petting his gun, smiling hungrily. Sam was sitting in the chair behind his desk, pipe belching a cloud of blue smoke, staring straight ahead of him at the place where Helwig had been standing.

"She is the daughter?" he asked, not looking at me.

"Been impersonating her mother for more than a year," I said. "All that jazz about Malinkov's magic is just that—jazz."

"You say she sent that warning note to me?"

"We don't know—just a guess. One of the women left it on a room-service tray. A waiter delivered it to the desk."

"But why should I be in danger?" Sam asked. "I don't get it. If she isn't my Charmian Brown none of these people has any conceivable reason for wanting to harm me."

"Ask Masters," I said. The coffee tasted good.

"A clever, clever kid," Masters said. "It's going to be a pleasure if I get the chance, Haskell." He aimed his gun at a point I imagined was directly between my eyes. Then he laughed and lowered it.

There was nothing to do but wait. For what? I asked myself. . . .

Things were happening in other places that I only learned about later.

First of all, Salinger, the absent watchdog on the nineteenth floor, was discovered in a linen closet a few doors down the hall from 19-B. He had been brutally slugged on the back of the head. A gun butt was Hardy's guess as the weapon. Salinger was out cold and the hospital offered nothing very hopeful as to when he might come to and tell his story. The guess was that one of the men, probably Helwig, had come out the door of 19-B and been promptly stopped by Salinger. While they argued, Masters had slipped out of one of the rooms down the line, sneaked up behind the detective, and let him have it. They'd dragged him into the linen closet and left him there—to die, for all they knew. Salinger's honor, if not his skull, was intact.

Our "pouter pigeon"—I'll never forget that one—was still working in high gear. Jerry Dodd told me later about that next fifteen minutes.

Mike Maggio had been traipsing all over the joint with the file cards Chambrun wanted. He finally caught up with the boss in the infirmary where they'd taken Salinger. Chambrun took the cards, went into Jerry Dodd's office with them, and proceeded to examine them. When he put them down his unshaven face was grim.

"I want a cop along with you, Jerry," he said. "Room 1922 is occupied by a man named Robin Miller. You know him?"

Jerry nodded. "Big wheel in airlines," he said. "Comes in about three times a year. Big spender. Something of a lush. We've escorted him politely out of the Grill and several other of the bars when he's gotten too noisy and obnoxious. He plays the call-girl routine quite a bit. I'm surprised we find space for him year after year."

Chambrun flipped the file card toward him. The letters *A* and *W* were on the card, indicating "alcoholic" and "woman-chaser." There was also a single sentence which read: "Recommended by G.B." G.B. were the initials of George Battle, who owns the Beaumont. That explained why Mr. Robin Miller had been allowed to return as a guest though his reputation with the staff was unsavory.

"What about him?" Jerry asked the boss.

"I want to get into his room."

"If he's out, a passkey will do it," Jerry said. "If he's in, ask and ye shall receive."

"I doubt it," Chambrun said. "How do you get past a chain-lock?"

"Quick or slow?" Jerry asked.

"Quick."

"Leave it to me," Jerry said.

I found out afterwards they have some kind of acid that eats right through the chain. Makes you wonder about the people all over town who count on chain-locks to keep out unwanted callers.

Jerry told me he got what was needed to obliterate the chain, and he and Chambrun and one of Hardy's cops went up to the nineteenth floor. Chambrun never once hinted at what he was up to.

Room 1922 had a "Do Not Disturb" sign hung on the knob. They knocked on the door. No answer. Jerry tried the passkey and the door opened just as far as the chain-lock would allow. An angry voice bellowed at them.

"What the hell's the matter with you? Can't you read? Bring your clean towels back some other time."

"It's not a maid," Chambrun said. "I'm the manager. I want to talk to you."

"For Godsake, it's not nine o'clock in the morning!" Miller said. "Come back some time when I'm awake."

"Now," Chambrun said.

"Knock it off," Miller said.

Chambrun gestured to Jerry. Ten seconds later they were in the room.

Jerry has seen some pretty peculiar things in the hotel. There was the Eastern potentate who tied his mistress to the bedpost each night and beat her with a rawhide whip. There would have been no trouble about it, because I guess the lady liked it, but the gentleman got in trouble when he tried to force a reasonably attractive chambermaid to submit to the same treatment. The girl screamed so loudly she could be heard through the soundproofed walls. There have been many equally dizzy ones. But Jerry wasn't prepared for what they found in Room 1922.

Mr. Robin Miller, friend of the owner, stood in the center of the room, stark naked. Cowering in a far corner, her dress half torn off, sporting a beautiful shiner, and holding a shiny steak knife like a dagger in her right hand, was Charmian Zetterstrom. A room-service dinner tray, which should have been removed long before, indicated where she'd acquired the knife.

Only Chambrun seemed completely unsurprised. He picked up an extra coverlet from the bed and handed it to Charmian. He didn't ask her anything.

"Put this around you, Miss Zetterstrom," he said. He turned to the cop. "Take the lady down to my office and have Miss Ruysdale attend to her. If anyone tries to stop you, use your gun. And stay on guard."

Charmian, Jerry said later, seemed to be in a state of shock. She didn't protest. She didn't say a word. She let Chambrun put the coverlet around her naked shoulders. She let the cop take her by the hand and lead her to the door. While all this was going on, Miller had picked up a terrycloth robe from a chair and covered his nakedness with it.

"Let's not have a lot of crap about this," he said, playing the big bluff for all it was worth. "The little tart came into my room uninvited and then she turned noble on me. I think you know I'm a friend of George Battle."

Parenthetically, I might say our owner, sitting on his golden beach on the Riviera, had some pretty strange friends, including Mr. Robin Miller and the Zetterstrom crew.

"What the hell brought you here? She didn't make a sound," Miller said, when Chambrun just stared at him out of narrow slits. "She was like some kind of zombie, but fought like a tiger."

"I came here because our records showed what kind of man you are, Mr. Miller. May I ask you, Mr. Miller, do most of your women come through the window from the ledge outside?"

"I don't know how she got in," Miller said. "I was asleep. I woke up suddenly and there she was, creeping toward the door. I figured her for some kind of hotel thief and I thought she might as well pay a good price for breaking into my room." He turned his head. "What the hell do you mean—window? It's nineteen floors straight down to the street. What kind of a nut would walk along that ledge?"

Chambrun, Jerry knew, was controlling white-hot anger.

"You will be out of this hotel in ten minutes, Mr. Miller," he said, "unless you want to face an attempted rape charge."

"The little bitch tried to cut me up with that steak knife she grabbed off the tray. *I'm* the aggrieved party, Chambrun. My room has been illegally entered. I—"

"Ten minutes," Chambrun said. "If you are not paying your bill at the desk by then you'll be placed under arrest."

"George Battle will hear about this!" Miller said.

"You can bet your life he will, Mr. Miller," Chambrun said, and left the room. . . .

In Sam Culver's apartment, we waited.

Sam sat at his desk, involved with his second pipe. Every once in a while I could hear him whistle soundlessly between his teeth. I have said that Sam is a man who's kept in wonderful physical shape for his years. I wouldn't want to tangle with him, even with a ten-year bulge in age. I wouldn't want to tangle with him or anyone else, to tell the truth. I take my action excitement out of the late-late movies. I'm like a million other guys around town; after your teens there isn't one chance in a million you'll ever have to tangle. You wouldn't know how. I was too young for the Korean war, too old for Vietnam.

Sam was something else again. He'd had a year's active duty in World War II and another solid hunk in Korea. He'd know how to fight for keeps, I thought, and it was certain that in Helwig and Masters we were up against two guys who would play it right out to the end of the line. I wondered if Sam was measuring the distance between himself and Masters. I wondered if he was cooking up some scheme; if he'd figured just the right moment to take a long-odds chance. I hoped I'd know how to fall in line if he started something.

The phone on his desk rang.

Helwig was instantly in the bedroom door. "You'll answer, Mr. Culver," he said. "You'll discourage anyone but Charmian who may be calling you. I'll be on the bedroom extension. Remember—play it your way and Masters and I have nothing to lose. We don't like being crossed." He disappeared back into the bedroom.

The phone kept ringing.

Sam, moving like an automaton, reached for the receiver. "Yes?" he said.

I know now that it was Chambrun, and I know now what he said.

"What's the matter with you, Sam? Hasn't Mark explained things? I want you down here."

"Let's say I don't feel like it," Sam said, in a flat voice.

"Perhaps you'll feel more like it when I tell you that we've found Charmian Zetterstrom."

"Oh," Sam said, as if it were a matter of no consequence to him.

"Aren't you at all interested to know what the plan was for murdering you, Sam? Aren't you at all interested in why the great impersonation—Charmian Two for Charmian One?"

"You have all those answers?" Sam asked.

"I have them, and I want you down here," Chambrun said.

Helwig was in the room, moving quickly toward Sam at the desk. "I'll take that phone," he said. "You and Haskell—over there against the wall."

I glanced at Masters. He wasn't fooling now about his aim. His hungry smile had widened into a frozen white gap in his face. Sam and I moved over against the wall of bookcases. Sam's eyes were cold and bright, but he made no offer to disobey.

Helwig picked up the phone. "Marcus Helwig here, Mr. Chambrun," he said. "Yes, we have been waiting here in the hope that Charmian would go to Mr. Culver."

"It's all over, Helwig," Chambrun said, on the other end.

I know now there was a good-sized gathering in the great man's office—Hardy, Jerry Dodd, Miss Ruysdale, who'd managed to get Charmian pinned together and a stiff brandy down her gullet. When Helwig identified himself Chambrun put his hand over the phone's mouthpiece and said the one word "Helwig." Hardy started for the door but Chambrun stopped him with a sharp "Wait!"

"The next step is just beginning, Mr. Chambrun," Helwig said. "I want you to listen quite carefully, because I don't have time to repeat my instructions twice."

"You have instructions for me?" Chambrun asked, his voice completely colorless.

"First, I would like to suggest that you don't assume

that by keeping me talking on the phone you have time to get someone up here. If someone knocks on the door or tries to get in some other way I promise you that either Mr. Culver or Mr. Haskell will be instantly dead."

"I have just stopped Lieutenant Hardy from leaving the room," Chambrun said. Our pouter pigeon had realized from the instant he heard Helwig's voice the nature of the next move.

"Second," Helwig said, "I would like you to put Charmian on the line for just long enough for me to make certain you weren't fooling Mr. Culver."

In the downstairs sanctum Chambrun held out the phone to Charmian. She came forward, reluctant, her blue eyes wide with fright.

"Speak to him," Chambrun said. "He wants to be sure you're here."

She took the phone, her hand shaking, but her voice was cool and clear. "I'm here, Marcus," she said. "I've told Mr. Chambrun and the lieutenant the whole story."

"I believe they taught you to pray in the convent, Charmian," Helwig said. His voice frightened me as I heard him speak. "I suggest that you start praying now that you never have the misfortune to encounter us again. Be good enough to put Mr. Chambrun back on the line."

Chambrun took back the phone. The others in his office watched and listened, as frozen as Sam and I were at the other end.

"We have one thing to gain, Mr. Chambrun—our freedom. We have nothing to lose by compounding our crime.

So what happens next depends entirely on how much you care about the life spans of Mr. Haskell and Mr. Culver."

"I'm listening," Chambrun said.

"You will be good enough," Helwig said, "to send for a rented limousine. When it is at the door you will call this room and tell us so. Then we will come out with Mr. Haskell and Mr. Culver. I will be walking behind one of them with a gun at his back, and Masters will be behind the other. We will go down in an elevator. We will walk across the lobby and out to the rented car. If there is one move, even a slightly suspicious move, to stop us, Mr. Haskell and Mr. Culver will fall dead in front of your eyes —and as many more as we can manage before the police shoot us down. When we get in the car you will not follow us. If we even imagine we are being followed your two friends will be shot to death where they sit. Is that all quite clear?"

"Quite clear," Chambrun said.

"You will send for the rented limousine?"

"After I have spoken to Mr. Haskell," Chambrun said.

"How long will it take to get the car here?"

"Fifteen minutes—after I have spoken to Mr. Haskell."

"Remember, if there is any attempt to get to us in this apartment, any attempt to stop us on the way out, it's all over."

"I'll remember," Chambrun said. "Put on Mr. Haskell."

"You," Helwig said to me, and held out the phone. I took it. "Hi," I said, sounding like a ten-year-old. "Mark, I'm sorry. I have no choice," Chambrun said.

"Yeah, yeah," I said. "Nice to have known you."

"In close quarters we might have a better chance," he said.

"Whatever that means."

"Tell Sam I'm sorry."

"Sure."

"You can inform Helwig I'll phone for his limousine now."

"You may ride in the front carriage," I said, feeling very sorry for myself. That limousine was likely to be our hearse.

The phone clicked off.

"You've heard enough to understand the plan," Helwig said to us. He had a gun now, and it looked as though he knew how to use it. "I want you to disabuse yourselves of the idea that when we leave here and find ourselves in the corridor, in the lobby, that you'll have a chance to run for it. One quick step away from us and you've had it."

"And we will have had it when you come to the end of your limousine ride," Sam said.

Helwig didn't answer. He moved over and sat on the edge of the desk by the phone, waiting for the word that the limousine had arrived. I looked at Sam. His face told me nothing. I found myself thinking about Shelda. I wish I'd thought to give Chambrun a message for her instead of my feeble attempts to crack wise. The silly little bitch, I loved her.

There was a clock on the mantel and I swear to God the second hand was racing like a mad thing. Fifteen minutes had never gone so fast in my whole life. While we waited, Masters had opened the coat closet by the front door and taken out Sam's raincoat and a topcoat.

And the phone rang.

"Yes," Helwig said. "Thank you."

Chambrun had delivered right on the button.

Masters took the raincoat and draped it over his right arm so that the gun in his hand was hidden. He stepped over behind Sam. Helwig imitated with the topcoat, and was behind me. I could feel his gun pressed hard in the middle of my back, which was now wet with sweat.

"Remember, gentlemen, one false move—" Helwig said. He didn't have to amplify. "Now, march."

Sam opened the door and he and Masters went out. I felt Helwig's gun jam into my back and I followed. I thought I was going to faint as I saw a maid coming down the hall toward us. Would they think she was some kind of Chambrun trick? But they smiled and nodded at her and she smiled and nodded back. Oh, baby, if you only knew, I thought.

We reached the elevators and I realized that my legs weren't going to take me across the lobby when we got there. The elevator door opened. It was a self-service car. Sam and I walked in and the others stood directly behind us. Masters, I think, pressed the down button.

I could feel my stomach coming up into my throat as the car plummeted down. And then it stopped. Someone else was coming aboard at a lower floor.

"One false move—" Helwig whispered.

We were going to look like damn fools, facing to the rear. I wondered if the passenger coming aboard would be someone I knew.

The elevator door didn't open.

"What's wrong?" Helwig said, sharply. "Press the down button again."

Out of the corner of my eye I could see Masters half turn to fumble with the button panel. Nothing happened. The car remained stationary. I turned my head to look at Sam. He was standing rigidly facing the rear wall, a little trickle of sweat running down his cheek. He was whistling tunelessly between his teeth.

Masters swore. "Damn thing doesn't want to move," he said.

Helwig's gun jammed hard into my back. "You know how this thing works, Haskell?"

"I can try," I said. "There's an emergency button."

"Get to it!"

It involved a curious shuffling of positions. Four of us seemed suddenly to crowd the car. I got turned around to face the control panel. Masters maneuvered Sam so that he was also facing front. I pressed the emergency button, but nothing happened. I jammed my finger against the down and up buttons. The car remained motionless.

Helwig was swearing under his breath in German. It sounded colorful.

Then something penetrated. Sam's little whistle had taken the form of a familiar little tune. I couldn't place it for a moment, and then suddenly it penetrated—"Dancing in the Dark."

I was staring at the control panel. Sweat was running down my back in small rivers. I was staring at the switch that said CAR LIGHTS. I took a look at Sam. His eyes seemed to be burning into me. He kept whistling that silly tune between his teeth—"Dancing in the Dark."

I threw the light switch and we were plunged into darkness.

"Sorry," I heard myself say.

Even as I was saying it, Sam must have exploded. My eardrums were shattered by a gunshot only inches away. Helwig seemed to be propelled violently back and away from me.

"Down, Mark! Down!" Sam was shouting.

I dropped flat on my face, trying to turn. If I was going to get it, I wanted to see it coming. There was nothing to see because the car was pitch-black. I was stepped on, kicked. I was at the bottom of a terrible struggle going on between Sam and the others. Another shot was fired and I could hear the bullet rip through the roof of the car. And then I felt the cold steel of a gun pressed against my cheek. I made a wild swinging gesture to knock it away and it went off.

I was still alive. And I was hanging onto Helwig's arm for dear life, twisting it with all the strength I had. I heard him cry out in pain.

And then there was a clicking sound and the lights came on. Sam was standing by the panel. He had a gun in his left hand. His right arm hung, crooked and useless, at his side. I could see blood pumping out of a wound near his right elbow. Masters lay, or half sat, in a corner of the car. Part of his face was gone. He looked very dead to me. I was sitting on top of Helwig, still twisting his arm. I saw his gun lying within easy reach. I picked it up and scrambled to my feet.

"Nice going," Sam said. "I was afraid you didn't know the tune."

From far away, as though it came from the other end of a tunnel, I heard Chambrun's voice shouting at us. "Mark! Sam!"

Sam lifted his head. "It's all right, Pierre!" he shouted. "Take it away."

We waited forever—probably ten seconds—and then the car started down. It stopped. The doors opened. Beyond us was the busy lobby, but directly in front of us was a small army—Chambrun, Jerry Dodd, Lieutenant Hardy, and half a dozen cops with guns drawn.

Chambrun's arms went around me and I grinned at him foolishly.

"My dear fellow," he said. "It was the only way I could see." He turned to Sam. "You were dead ducks, Sam, if they ever got you out of the hotel. There was no way to stop them. They meant exactly what they said. I thought if the car was stopped, it would be the one thing they weren't prepared for. It was a chance—the only chance. I tried to hint to Mark. I told him that in close quarters you might have a better chance."

I giggled foolishly. "It never occurred to me that meant

anything," I said.

Hardy and his men were in the elevator, attending to a dead man and a prisoner.

"We'd better have Doc Partridge look at that arm of yours," Chambrun said to Sam. . . .

A little while later we were in Chambrun's office—Sam, with his arm in a black-silk sling; Lieutenant Hardy; Miss Ruysdale, plying Chambrun with some fresh Turkish coffee which seemed to make a new man of him; and, huddled in the big armchair by Chambrun's desk, Charmian Zetterstrom, looking like a twelve-year-old child.

The girl told us her story, most of it in a dull monotone, staring past Chambrun at the paneled wall. Her first memories were of the convent on the Greek mainland. She and her sister Heidi were taken there as babies. The Baron, it seemed, had a fear about children. They were accidents he wanted to forget. The girls never laid eyes on him, although he lived until young Charmian was eighteen years old. The Baroness, the original Charmian Brown, had some feeling for her daughters. She came to see them at the convent perhaps once every month or six weeks. As Charmian grew up she found her mother to be an exciting, glamorous, very wonderful person. There was a special tie between them because it was obvious, even when she was a small child, that young Charmian was going to be a physical double for her mother.

When the Baron died, the two girls were promptly brought to the Island to live. There were very few visitors or parties in those days. The Baroness was already fighting the cancer that would eventually kill her.

"I really got to know my mother then," the girl said. "She spent hours talking to me about her life, most of it very bitter. As she told it, she had been forced into all kinds of excesses and immoralities by the Baron. Now that it was past her, no longer possible, she described it all with loathing and resentment. The chief targets of her hatred were all the men in the world who had had anything to do with her. I should have realized that she was sick, paralyzed with fright at the thought of dying, trying to place the blame somewhere else for the kind of life she'd lived, as though that would save her from eternal damnation. I didn't see it that way. I believed her. I sympathized with her."

The girl turned her wide blue eyes toward Sam. "The prime object of her hatred was you, Mr. Culver. You had destroyed her career in Hollywood. You had prevented her from living a decent, successful life. You had driven her into the Baron's world. You were right of course, Mr. Chambrun. The Island was a haven for German war criminals. Dr. Malinkov gave them new faces and they stayed there until they were able to go out into the world again, unrecognizable. My mother was subjected to their interim pleasures. She felt she was responsible for sending them out into the world, free to continue their crimes. She blamed you, Mr. Culver. You were an obsession with her. You must be punished—she told me this day after day, week after week. I began to see you as some kind of monster. As my mother's time to die came closer, she began to work on me. You see, the Baron knew I was his child. He wasn't sure about Heidi, so he disinherited her. I would have all the Zetterstrom money and power, my mother told me. I would be the most powerful woman in the world. It was pretty heady stuff. I must make her one promise. When she was gone I would hunt down Sam Culver and destroy him. She kept at it and at it and I promised her. I wanted to do it!

"After my mother died it took a long time to straighten out the business affairs. As you've been told, I had begun to impersonate her with some success. Marcus had reasons for not making her death public. He wanted certain investments changed, certain deals made, before it was known and the Zetterstrom fortune became an estate for which he was accountable. I trusted him—why not? My mother and father had trusted him all their lives.

"In all the time it took to work out those arrangements Marcus kept reminding me of my promise to my mother. Before I could make a life of my own I had to settle with Sam Culver. And eventually Marcus had a scheme. We'd come to New York and establish contact with Sam Culver. We would make him believe that I was his Charmian, kept young and beautiful by Malinkov's skills. He *had* kept my mother looking extraordinarily young, you know. But not—not as young as I am. I was to attract Sam Culver to his Charmian all over again. I was to get him to the point where he would be pleading with me to become my lover—again, as he would think. Then there would be a party for him, to celebrate our coming together. At that party, Mr. Culver, you were to be poisoned. You would die very quickly, writhing in agony, and I would hold you and whisper the truth to you: Charmian Brown had paid you off!" The girl drew a deep breath. None of us moved or spoke.

"And so we left the Island for the first time, stopping in London on the way. Heidi knew about the plan. She kept pleading with me to reject it. She and Peter were in love. They wanted a life completely separated from the Zetterstrom madness. Heidi had no part in the scheme against you, Mr. Culver, but knowing about it she felt she was an accessory. She pleaded and begged, day after day, for me to give it up. But I had been hypnotized by my mother into believing in the principle of an eye for an eye. It was just and proper that Sam Culver should pay for what he'd done. And Marcus and Masters and Clara kept pushing me that way. I thought how extraordinarily loyal to my mother they were.

"So we got here—and I was instantly in trouble. I didn't recognize Stephen Wood. How could I? I had never seen him or his brother in my life."

"But you remembered so much detail," Sam said, his voice hollow. "Exact words spoken, exact actions."

"Oh, I was schooled in that, Mr. Culver. My mother had forgotten nothing. She told me every detail, every word spoken between you that night."

"Did she tell you the real truth about my father?"

"She told it to me both ways," Charmian said. "I don't

know which was the truth."

I heard Sam let out his breath in a long, quavering sigh.

"The minute we reached our rooms upstairs after I'd made my two blunders in the lobby, Marcus was at me, telling me things about Mr. Culver, how I could retrieve the moment of passing him by. But do you know, something had happened to me. In the time we'd spent in London I'd seen people living normally, happily. And the glimpse I'd had of you, Mr. Culver—you didn't look like a monster. Suddenly I wanted to give up. Marcus was outraged. He had me send for Mr. Chambrun to arrange for the party. You came instead, Mark. You were pleasant, and charming, and relaxed. I began to think I was a character out of some kind of gilded nightmare. The whole project was unreal. But Marcus forced me on.

"I sent for Mr. Culver. I was ready for him. I convinced him I was his Charmian Brown. But I thought I saw a way to make Marcus' scheme unworkable. I thought if you refused to come to the party, that would be that. And so I—I told you a different story about your father, Mr. Culver. I thought you would hate me so much for it, you wouldn't dream of coming to the party. In the middle of that moment, Mr. Chambrun and Mark came to tell me about poor little Puzzi.

"After that it became a real nightmare. Marcus and Masters had been listening. They knew what I was up to. They talked together while they waited for you all to go, and Heidi overheard them. You weren't to be the only victim, Mr. Culver. I was number two on the list. I was to be caught by the police as your poisoner. I would be convicted and executed. And then, by the terms of my father's will, the entire Zetterstrom fortune would be divided among his faithful servants—Marcus Helwig, Masters, Clara, and Dr. Malinkov. If I did not provably die at their hands, the money was theirs. And so I was to commit a murder and they would see to it I was caught.

"Heidi got to tell me a little of this before we were interrupted by Clara. We sat there, frozen, while a waiter served us tea. I managed to slip a note on the tea table for Mr. Culver. I was terrified. I realized I was a prisoner. I had no one to turn to. Then Malinkov asked if Heidi would get a prescription filled for him. She was eager to go; she wanted to find Peter. Maybe he could think of a way out for us. And so she went—and Masters was waiting for her. Stephen Wood had played into their hands by killing Puzzi. Masters made Heidi's murder look like the work of the same man. Moving the body away from the nineteenth floor was dangerous, so Masters borrowed Peter's clothes. If anyone saw him they would think it was Peter. Peter, like the rest of us, was expendable.

"I was no longer the Baroness, or the heiress. I was their prisoner. I'd destroyed their plan and I knew about Heidi. Now they had to face out the police investigation and get me away, back to the Island. I wasn't let out of their sight. If I opened my mouth to you, Mr. Chambrun, or to the police, I wouldn't get the words spoken before I was dead. Marcus was always at my elbow. I did manage to leave a note for you, Mr. Chambrun. Did you ever find it?"

"I found it, but not for a long time," Chambrun said. "Like an idiot, I played with it for hours before I opened it and looked at it. By the time I got to your suite you'd gone."

Charmian shuddered. "It—it was the most awful experience of my whole life," she said. "I'm terrified of heights. But it was the only way. I crept out on that ledge—and I froze. I couldn't move away and I couldn't go back in. It seemed as though I stood there, pressed back against the wall of the building for hours. But, at last, I found I could move inch by inch along the ledge, never looking down, because that could have been the end. I—I got around the corner of the building and in through the first window I found. It took me into the room with that incredible man! I couldn't get away from him—I couldn't get to the phone. I had begun to think my only hope was to give into him—when you arrived."

"One of the techniques of running a hotel," Chambrun said. "You get to know your people. Anyone on that floor but Robin Miller would have helped you, and called my office. So you had to be in his room." He lit a cigarette. "Masters and Helwig were desperate when they found you were gone. They had to find you before you told us your story, and from talking to us they knew you hadn't reached us yet. Their main mistake was, they felt certain you'd go to Sam to warn him instead of coming to me. They had Sam as a hostage. They were certain they could use him to get out of the hotel if it came to that. Mark gave them an extra card to play."

"I think they had a plane chartered somewhere," Charmian said. She sank down in her chair.

"But their position was hopeless," Sam said. "I knew the truth about them."

"You'd never have gotten to tell it," Chambrun said. "If Charmian had come to your apartment you'd have been shot, Sam, and Charmian, in all probability, would have gone out the window, an apparent suicide. Then Helwig & Company would have had a long, lugubrious story for us, about a mother-nurtured revenge. They might have gotten away with it. But when she didn't come, when we got to her first, they had you and Mark as hostages. They would almost certainly have gotten out of the hotel. We wouldn't have dared move to stop them. Fortunately, I had my thought about the elevator. If they got you out of the hotel you'd almost certainly have been killed when they arrived wherever they were going."

Charmian leaned back in her chair, covering her face with her hands.

Sam Culver walked over and stood beside her. "I'd like to help you, Charmian," he said, gently. "It might make up for some of the past."

Chambrun looked at me, and then at Jerry and Miss Ruysdale. "Let's not dawdle around here all morning," he said. "We've got a hotel to run."